ALL THAT REMAINS

ALL THAT REMAINS

(INSPIRED BY A TRUE EVENT)

DAVE HART

ALL THAT REMAINS

iUniverse books may be ordered through booksellers or by contacting:

iUniverse
1663 Liberty Drive
Bloomington, IN 47403
www.iuniverse.com
844-349-9409

ISBN: 978-1-6632-3432-2 (sc)
ISBN: 978-1-6632-3433-9 (e)

Print information available on the last page.

iUniverse rev. date: 01/06/2022

Also from the Author...

Tipping Point by Dave Hart © 2021 iUniverse Publishing, Inc.

All the Pretty Pieces by Dave Hart ©2020 iUniverse Publishing, Inc.

Search for the Missing Hunter by Dave Hart © 2020 iUniverse Publishing, Inc.

Adventures Along the Jersey Shore by Dave Hart & John Calu Copyright © 2015 Plexus Publishing, Inc.

- *The Treasure of Tucker's Island*
- *Mystery of the Jersey Devil*
- *Secret of the Painted Rock*
- *Lost Mission of Captain Carranza*
- *Riddle in the Sand*
- *Spirits of Cedar Bridge*
- *Storm Warnings*

Trenton: *a novel* by John P. Calu and David A. Hart Copyright © 2010 Plexus Publishing, Inc.

For more information about Dave Hart's work visit-
https://hartcalu.com/

http://www.plexuspublishing.com/Books/Trenton.shtml

Film/Video
http://www.johnhartpatriot.com/HART/John_Hart.html

Music
http://www.wavesonamillpond.com/index.html

For Frank J. Pinto III
A multi-talented musician and singer whose gift of song
has been instrumental in giving a
melodic voice to my words

Acknowledgments

Many thanks to Victoria Ford my trusty and ever-resourceful editor

1

I'm not the kind of guy who gets off on attending funerals—my own included. Paying my last respects to family and friends was not something I relished doing. But this occasion was not like that. This was a funeral service for a total stranger.

Mainly I was at Keppler's Funeral Home because a prospective client insisted I attend before she would discuss important details regarding a case for which my creative investigative skills were being considered. She strongly suggested I go to the service to reflect upon the parting comments offered by grieving colleagues and acquaintances of the deceased. The exercise, she assured me, would provide proper context for what I'd be getting myself into, should I decide to take the assignment.

Normally, I wouldn't nibble on such a ridiculous morsel. But the fact that the funeral service was for my prospective client's first husband made it seem salacious to my way of thinking and naturally attractive to my professional curiosity. And to be honest, I found myself, for the moment at least, in the throes of a protracted financial dry spell—of which my well-meaning, long-suffering secretary reminded me almost daily.

Standing in the funeral parlor in my one decent dark suit, I tried to appear downcast and consoling while casually eavesdropping and silently observing a crowd of unfamiliar mourners. It wasn't a good fit. With every smile and polite nod, I groused inwardly. How little I actually knew about the deceased or, for that matter, the impending case! I knew only what Mrs. Rose Lynwood chanced to share with me during our brief telephone conversation the day before yesterday.

Over the phone she sounded like an educated woman, up in years. She was calling from out of state on the strength of an unnamed referral source. My curiosity was fueled when she hinted at some alleged personal grievance, in which a matter of public interest might also be entangled. It sounded far too good for an eager PI named McKenzie Cole to ignore, and she knew it.

Mrs. Lynwood had happened to mention that Ryan Hardwick, the deceased, had worked in local law enforcement most of his adult life. That would explain the numerous blue uniforms milling about. Long divorced, she admitted to me that their wedded bliss lasted a mere six months before it fell apart. Amazingly, that was forty-four years ago. Both had apparently remarried, enjoyed successful careers, and savored their second bites at the apple. So, why the sudden renewed interest in her first husband's life? That's what I needed to find out.

Trying to look inconspicuous at a stranger's funeral as a guy with an innate distain for funerals was tougher than I'd imagined, and I'd imagined the worst. For one thing, I couldn't shake the feeling that I was being watched by an awkwardly curious man in a rumpled gray suit. Whether I was sitting alone in quiet contemplation in the rear of the chapel, or hiding among a cluster of gossiping mourners, everywhere I turned, his eyes seemed to be trained on me.

It made me feel uneasy, as though he could sense I didn't belong there. And I didn't. I looked around for the nearest exit. When I turned back, he was in my face, and the brewery he had come from came with him.

"You a friend of the deceased?" he asked in a dry, nasally tone, squinting his beady eyes as he scrutinized mine. On his face he wore three-day-old stubble proudly.

On a younger man it might have been considered trendy. On a man roughly my age, it hinted at a more pronounced problem. His white dress shirt was open at the collar, revealing a small blue six-pointed star tattooed on his neck. *If anyone looks out of place here, it's him*, I thought. My gut suggested he was either an off-duty cop badly in need of sleep (among other things) or the funeral director's smarmy assistant. If a cop, he had the swagger but lacked the commanding rigidity. If the assistant, he needed coffee and a wardrobe upgrade.

"What do *you* think?" I replied, sounding politely noncommittal.

"I didn't think he had any friends," he said, glancing at the memorial photo in the front of the room. "Only 'brothers in blue.'"

"Like you?" I inquired, operating on instinct while conducting a little fishing expedition of my own.

"There are worse things," he deflected with a chuckle. "I'm Shelly," he said. He didn't specify first or last name, as if I should know. He extended his hand. It felt clammy and limp.

"I don't recall seeing you around. You from the area?" he continued awkwardly, trying to get any information he could out of me in our confined meeting space.

"I'm from out of state. Trenton, actually. Name's Cole."

"You've come a long way for a brother's funeral, friend. You two must have been close."

"Not really," I replied. "Worked a case together years back. Thought I owed him."

'Uh, huh."

"The paper attributed the cause of death to 'heart failure'. Did he have a heart condition?"

"Could have," he replied with a sardonic half smile. "From an overabundance of brotherly love if you ask me."

A slender, veiled woman dressed in black quietly entered from the anteroom and made her way toward the center of the chapel, carrying an ornate reliquary urn.

"Excuse me," Shelly apologized abruptly. "Duty calls," he added, popping a breath mint into his mouth. He scurried off to join several uniformed officers swarming around the widow like worker bees around their queen.

When Reverend Roy stepped forward to begin the final prayer for the departed, I made my exit through the rear of the chapel.

2

I had never been to Cross Point, Pennsylvania before making my tortured appearance at Keppler's Funeral Parlor. Tucked away, across the Delaware River in the northeastern corner of Bucks County, Cross Point was located about fifty-six miles from my office in downtown Trenton. While I was less than eager to make the trip, for various reasons, it turned out to be a beautiful Wednesday in early June, the perfect kind of day for a pleasant ride through Pennsylvania farm country with the top down on my prized 1966 Jaguar XKE.

I had heard of the college town, mainly because it was the home of the Buckland State Badgers. A small state-funded school, Buckland concentrated almost exclusively on a solid liberal arts curriculum for educators. I knew several former Badgers living in the Trenton area. One of them was Nick Falcone, the loquacious bartender who served drinks nightly at Jake's Joint, my hometown watering hole. Aha—that just might explain where my Lynwood referral came from.

As planned, after the service I headed straight for the Lynwood residence. Sycamore Avenue was a broad thoroughfare that intersected Main Street at the southern end of town. Seventeen Sycamore Street was a charming white Victorian with high gables and a wide portico extending halfway around the front of the house. Rose Lynwood was sitting on the porch in a wicker rocking chair, waiting for me with a pitcher of iced tea. She motioned for me to pull into the driveway, which I did before joining her on the porch.

"The Sycamores are shedding this time of year," she shouted as I hustled up the walk. "If you'd parked that classic ragtop of yours on the street, you'd have had one heck of a cleaning bill. Mind you, that's not the sort of thing I would reimburse you for."

"Then I appreciate the driveway courtesy all the more," I said with a warm smile, matching the one she flashed beneath a set of cerulean eyes. I guessed her age to be just north of seventy. At least I'd guessed the elderly part right from our phone conversation. But nothing could have prepared me for the total package. Neat, petite and well groomed, Rose Lynwood projected the epitome of dignity and class. Light on the makeup with not a strand of gray hair out of place, she was dressed in a zebra-striped sundress like she was going to a Sunday church social. Grace and elegance were two words that came to mind as she held out her hand genteelly for me to take. I sat down in the loveseat next to her, wondering what it was like to court a gal like Rose Lynwood in her prime.

"You're not as tall as I pictured you, Mr. Cole. But that distinctive moustache of yours certainly adds a bit of stature and, dare I say, an air of mystery."

Rose Lynwood didn't pull her punches. Clearly, I had to be on my guard.

"Not everyone in this business has the bone structure of Basil Rathbone," I replied with a sheepish grin. "Unfortunately, some of us fall into the Columbo camp."

"Ah, a wit. I like that. Tea?" she offered without skipping a beat.

I loosened my tie. "Thanks. Most folks call me Mac."

"Of course they do. I hope you don't mind mint, Mr. Cole." She ignored the suggestion. "It's kind of a sugar substitute for me. The leaves are from my own garden, in the back. It's my one remaining passion. Digging in the dirt keeps me grounded, and the soil here is splendid for giant sycamores, peppermint leaves, and a great many other things."

"Delicious," I said after tasting. And it was, indeed. "It makes me wonder, what were some of the other passions you've given up along the way?" I added flirtatiously.

Rose Lynwood blushed ever so slightly, letting her sparkling blues eyes speak what her lips dared not say. "So, tell me—what did you learn at the Hardwick service?"

"Without knowing more about the case, nothing of any consequence, I'm afraid.

Although I must admit, based on the comments from some of the mourners who eulogized him, that Hardwick was known for his creative turns of phrase. 'A day without a good dump is like a day without sunshine' had to be one of the more colorful ones I heard today."

"Yes, he certainly had a way with words. He used to like to tell people my second husband, Carter Lynwood, who was a well-educated man, mind you, and later became the provost at BSC, had 'more degrees than a thermometer.'"

"Yogisms," I said with a chuckle, although I don't believe she caught the reference. "I'll wager that one was said to hide his jealousy."

"I'll wager you are quite correct about that, Mr. Cole."

Rose Lynwood paused to pour herself a glass of tea. "Was there any talk of the past?" she inquired, still looking down.

7

"Your name never came up," I replied, thinking I was reading between the lines.

"How about his early law enforcement days—strange cases, notorious crimes, things like that?"

"There certainly was some of that going around," I acknowledged. "Good-natured stuff, it seemed to me, a lot of joking and innuendo—like you might hear at a PBA meeting or bowling alley. I imagine cops are coached not to let loose with too much of that in public."

"The 'boys in blue' certainly are a tight fraternity," she added coyly. "Maybe they're just as sensitive to those things as the general public. They are only human, are they not?"

"Yeah. I guess you don't spend—what, forty?—years in uniform without a good story or two to tell. But maybe the darker ones are better kept quiet."

"Forty-four years, to be exact," she corrected. "Thanks in large part to his daddy."

"Come to think of it, there was some mention of his old man. Wasn't he the police chief?"

"Lionel Hardwick. Cross Point's finest of the finest. He's the one who got Ryan into law enforcement—starting with the campus security job at BSC. Did anyone happen to mention anything about that?"

"No. When was that?"

"1977," she said with some trepidation, looking off into the distance. "The year we were married."

I shook the ice cubes gently, then set my tumbler down on the glass-topped wicker table positioned between us. The rap of glass on glass interrupted Rose's nostalgic thoughts, as I had hoped. Such pleasant chatter with this charming lady was all very nice, but it wasn't getting me anywhere. I still had no idea what her problem was or why she needed my services.

She must have been reading my thoughts, or else she'd reached the same conclusion. Either way, Rose took a deep breath and exhaled slowly. Looking directly into my eyes, she said, "You've been very patient with me, Mr. Cole, so let me cut to the chase for you."

Again she hesitated. "Have you ever heard the name Sonja Olson in your travels? You may have to search deep in your memory, because the name goes way back."

I sat for a moment, thinking hard. The name sounded Scandinavian. *Maybe Sonja Olson is a skier or an ice skater*, I thought. *Perhaps an Olympian? A fashion model or international actress?* When I was certain I couldn't place the name, I confessed, "No, I can't say I recall hearing that name before."

"That doesn't surprise me," Rose admitted, pursing her lips, "because you're not from around here, and I don't think the story got much national attention back then. Lord knows the school and the local police did everything they could to keep the lid on it."

Rose sat back in her chair and tented her hands as she continued.

"Sonja Olson was a student at Buckland State College in 1977. A music major, studying for her master's degree. She was brutally murdered on campus. The case has never been solved. I believe my first husband, the late Ryan Hardwick, murdered her."

3

Speechless. Rose Lynwood's unexpected remarks rendered me speechless. Sitting there in her rocker, calm and composed, she watched closely as I struggled to find an appropriate response, as if any such response were possible.

"That's quite an accusation, Rose. Did Ryan tell you that when he was alive?"

"Of course not."

"Then how do you know?"

"Because it *ruined* our marriage."

"Lots of things can ruin a marriage," I ventured with a sigh. "Mine fell apart over a wristwatch I purchased from Macy's. At least that's what I tell myself. But believing your husband is a murderer beats buyer's remorse in spades."

She studied my face. I gauged my expression landed somewhere between bewildered and blown away. Her own face remained granite, perfectly still and eerily serene.

"You don't believe me, do you, Mr. Cole?"

"It's not that I don't believe you; I'm in shock. Forty-four years is a hell of a long time to carry that burden around with you. Why now? And why tell me? What do want me to do about it?"

"I want you to prove he did it."

"How?"

"You're an investigator. Investigate."

"Why does that matter now? He's dead."

"It matters to me."

"Maybe, but it's really a police matter. I'm not even sure the police records are still around. We're talking almost fifty years ago."

"They are."

"What, on microfilm? How long does that stuff hold up, anyway? They're just plastic strips."

"No. Paper files. I'm sure of it."

"How do you know that?"

"Because my daughter inquired."

"Well, there you go. You don't need me. Have her go over to the Cross Point police station and retrieve the records for you."

"We tried that."

"And?"

"The police refused. They said the case was still under investigation because they continue to receive new leads about the case almost daily."

"All the more reason it's a police matter, Rose."

"No. It's been the same way for four decades, Mr. Cole. Nothing but stonewalling from the authorities. It began on day one, with Chief Lionel Hardwick. With him and Ryan gone, I thought things might loosen up, but apparently not. That's why I called you. I need a professional. Someone who knows his way around the red tape."

"And *I* was the best choice you could come up with?"

"I needed someone with a fresh perspective. An outsider."

"You mean someone not in Hardwick's pocket."

Rose Lynwood's eyes lit up like fireworks. "You're beginning to see the big picture, Mr. Cole."

"What makes you think they'll turn over those old documents to me?"

"I don't know. Call it professional courtesy or personal persuasion. Charisma, maybe."

"You referring to me?"

"That's what my daughter Rachel says about you."

"Rachel Lynwood? Sorry, I don't recognize that name either.

"But she knows yours. She's the one who found you."

"And just how did Rachel find me? I'm not listed in the Cross Point Yellow Pages, that I know of, unless it's under the heading 'Suckers For Hire.'"

"Don't kid yourself, Mr. Cole. Finding you was easy. Nick Falcone. He and Rachel went to BSC together. They dated for a while and stayed in touch. I always liked Nick. A real charmer. Funny, though, I have a hard time picturing him as a bartender. I always thought he wanted to be an actor."

"Believe me, he does his best acting behind the bar."

At that, Rose chuckled. A wan smile appeared on her lips. She lifted the icy pitcher. More tea?"

I held out my glass. I would have preferred Jack Daniels on the rocks, but it wasn't on her tea tray.

"So that's why you had me go to the funeral? To rub elbows with Ryan's boys, endear myself to them? Well, I did my best to avoid interaction with nearly everyone, except for this one annoying guy who seemed to make it his business to know everybody there. Otherwise, I played the part of 'fly on the wall,' as instructed. Even Nick would have been proud."

"Which is why I couldn't attend, you understand. I would have stuck out. You did just what I'd hoped you'd do: be seen. Get noticed, but remain anonymous. Should it ever come to it, someone may recall seeing you there and think of you as a regular part of the Hardwick team."

"Right now I'm feeling a bit overwhelmed and still very much in the dark, Rose. Maybe you should start at the beginning for me?"

"The beginning? It's simple. Ryan was the first one on the scene. He found Sonja Olson's naked, battered body before anyone else arrived."

"That doesn't make him the killer."

"You don't understand. He'd been working security at the college for less than a year. His father got him the job. I worked in the bursar's office. That's how we met. We'd been married for a little over three months when it happened."

"Go on."

"The event changed him. Changed our marriage. He was different. He became introspective and withdrawn, except ..."

"He was unable to perform his husbandly duties?"

"Quite the opposite, Mr. Cole. Look, despite how I may appear to you, I'm no prude. I was as promiscuous as any girl coming of age in the seventies. I just wasn't into bondage and that sort of thing."

"And Ryan was?"

"Before the incident, no. After, yes, and more."

"And you think the two are related?"

"Sonja's hands were bound and she was gagged with a tee shirt. Ryan would blindfold me, tie me up and gag me."

"Was she raped?"

Rose looked away.

"Was Sonja raped?" I repeated.

"Not according to most of the local papers at that time and since. But, who knows? I've never seen the actual police report. I don't know anyone who has. The police controlled the media, and back then Lionel Hardwick *was* the police. After JFK and Watergate, could anyone trust what they read in the newspapers? And now with the internet, it's worse. Everything is sensationalized or slanted."

"Did Ryan hit you, Rose?"

Again she looked away. "What do you think?"

"Is that why the marriage fell apart?"

She grabbed my hands. Tears pooled in her once twinkling eyes. "I need to know, Mr. Cole. I'll pay you whatever you ask. But I've got to know before I die."

4

It was early evening when I left the Lynwood residence, my bladder brimming with iced tea. I could have trekked the hour-plus back to Trenton but chose not to. Instead I phoned my secretary and had her book a room for me overnight in town. Leave it to Mary Porter to find a lovely B&B on Main Street—and one that fit into our dwindling budget—quaintly named the Happy Orchard Inn.

Although I'd reluctantly accepted Rose Lynwood's offer to take the case, I still wasn't quite sure what she wanted me to do: prove Ryan Hardwick killed Sonja Olson, or prove that he didn't? Closure, if that's all she was after, seemed anti-climactic to me, whether or not the police were complicit in a coverup back then. Ryan Hardwick was dead. If he didn't do it, that meant the killer was still out there. He'd been given a free pass. Maybe that didn't sit well with Rose Lynwood. I know it didn't sit right with me.

Either way, I needed to do my homework. Getting a feel for the town of Cross Point seemed like a good start. I also needed to visit the Buckland State campus in order to get the lay of the land. I needed to try and cast myself back there some forty-four years and locate students and others who may have known Sonja. I needed to learn all the dirty secrets quickly and separate the facts from the expanding legends that had grown up around the horrific event. In short, I needed to get to the truth, and that window of opportunity was closing fast—perhaps forever.

I realized I was going to need help. Private investigators, by design, occupy a lonely profession. Few family members and fewer friends come with the territory. Generally, the fewer colleagues or associates, the better. After all, the job calls for keeping things, well, private.

That I managed to operate with just one fulltime employee, a dedicated secretary who'd been with me from the start and endured the peaks and valleys, was a plus. To her credit, Mary Porter had never wavered in her commitment to the job, or to me. That made it much easier for me to function independently when I needed to be discreet.

As a rule, law enforcement personnel and private investigators don't get along. Relationships tend to be adversarial, as was the case with Trenton Police Detective Greg O'Malley and me. Some of the estrangement had to do with perception, as well as money. Cops are public servants sworn to serve and protect, paid by taxpayer dollars from a tight city budget, further restricted by copious rules and voluminous regulations.

PIs, on the other hand, are limited only by the largess of their paying clients, and, while guided by a vague set of common principles and professional ethics, many—myself included—have been known to push things to extremes. The distrust between the two camps manifests as competition, since both teams are basically trying to accomplish the same thing: get to the truth, then let justice prevail. But each side can have a very different idea of "justice."

Because this case involved a murder, I believed strongly that, however cold, the case remained a police matter first. Ergo, an ally on the police force would prove invaluable. Over the years I had had the good fortune to work with Trenton's venerable Chief Bill Perkins. Though neither would go so far as to use the word "friend," we had helped each other, directly and indirectly, during some tough times, while managing to maintain good boundaries. That sort of working relationship can build improbable bonds.

After I checked into my clean and tidy room at the Happy Orchard Inn, I went down to the lobby to use the pay phone. Fortuitously, the Inn had a working coin-operated payphone. Given the nature of my question for Bill, it was best not to use cell phones. I inserted my tower of quarters and dialed.

"Hello, Shirley Mae. It's me, Mac."

"Sweet Jesus, Mac. Whatchall doin', callin' on this line? You forget to pay your phone bill?"

"It's a long story, Shirley Mae, and unfortunately this is a long-distance call. So if you don't mind, could you please patch me right through to the Chief?"

"If he's still here, you bet. Y'all keep your britches on, hear me, sugar?"

"I'll do my best, sweet cheeks."

After a brief silence, Perkins' melodious voice came on the line.

"Well, well, well," he intoned. "Chamber of Commerce finally run you out of town?"

"You might want to leave the jokes to Billy Crystal," I said. I'd come to understand his sardonic humor was also a form of friendliness.

"Hey, I must be moving up. You could've said Redd Foxx."

"Not a fit. You only look like him."

Perkins chuckled. "Flattery will get you nowhere."

"I'm counting on that, but I need a favor anyway."

"That explains the unofficial-official phone line. Should I start planning for early retirement?"

"Only if you're not the man I think you are."

"Now I know I'm in trouble. If I recall, you played your sole remaining gold brick during your last case when O'Malley saved your ass from getting whooped by that gargantuan wrestler."

"I'm sure that's how Detective O'Malley tells it, but we both know Dumbo the Elephant was down for the count long before O'Malley showed up with your boys."

"I'll have to remind him. So, what do you need the TPD for this time?"

"I need your help to get police records on an old murder case from a precinct out here in Podunk County."

"How old?"

"Happened around the time you were a cadet at the academy."

"That old, huh? And why would I want to do that?"

"To catch the killer."

"Unsolved. Four decades later. Are the records still around? Is the guy even still around?"

"I don't know about the killer, but I believe the records are, because my client's Open Public Records Act requests have been denied by the local authorities. They claim the case remains open."

"And that's where the TPD comes in?"

"They don't call you the chief for nothing. If the case truly is still open, TPD just ran across some new information that may be pertinent."

"We did?"

"You did. But, because the crime happened so long ago, you need to review the original reports and refamiliarize yourself with the case before determining whether the tip is relevant enough to take to Cross Point PD."

"Why wouldn't the locals just send their own man down here, or take a statement from us over the phone?"

"Manpower. It's a small town with a small force. Lots of jaywalkers and kitties stuck in trees. Also, I'm guessing they won't want to, because I just came from the funeral of the last of the initial investigators involved with the case. I doubt anybody else on the force today gives a damn."

"Then why block the OPRA requests?"

"Because the people in charge back then ruled with an iron fist and left specific instructions never to release the material to the public. These folks are drones, Bill. Out here, you don't rock the boat. You leave the oars on the shore and let the current carry you."

"You think they're hiding something, Mac? Maybe Internal Affairs should be alerted?"

"Too late for that, Bill. IA would say it's ancient history, closed or not. We need to restir the pot."

"Sounds like there's nothing left in the pot to stir?"

"How about a probable witness who claims to have important information regarding the case?"

Admittedly, "probable witness" was stretching the truth a bit, but I felt somewhat justified because at least Rose Lynwood's recollections constituted a firsthand account—not of the crime itself, but of the related deviant behavior of a person involved in the case.

"Evidentiary information?"

"No. Not that I can determine. But I believe it to be credible."

"That's not very convincing, Mac. On a case this old, memories can be a liability."

"I agree, Bill, but you'll have to trust me on this one. I've vetted the witness myself. She's rock solid."

"She the client?"

"Let's just say she's willing to invest my time and her money on this."

"You said 'probable witness.' Does she have a vested interest in the outcome?"

"Only that justice prevails. Same as you and me."

"Okay, Mac. I'll see what I can do. But we'll have to do it my way. Get the particulars over to Shirley Mae. Then, give me a couple of days. Assuming they can locate the reports and decide to grant us access, you'll have to come down to the station to look them over. The documents must stay here. I need to maintain some measure of the 'blue code' if only for the sake of my own conscience."

"Will do, Bill. And Thanks. I owe you one."

5

While the TPD worked on their end, I was eager to get my education started, so I ordered takeout from McKenna's Café across the street. Then I settled back in my room to enjoy the chicken Caesar salad wrap, Lay's potato chips and a bottle of Poland Spring water while I read over the two brochures I grabbed from the rack in the lobby.

The first brochure provided an interesting history of the Happy Orchard Inn. Originally a farmhouse constructed in 1870 and the site of a popular apple orchard, the building was converted into an Inn at the end of WWII. The three-story house contained eight guest rooms: two to a floor, with a shared bathroom between them. The current owners, Hugh Bennett and Mark Abrams, both former New York stockbrokers, purchased the Inn in 2008 shortly after the financial market crash.

With the college in recess for summer, currently only three of the oak-paneled rooms were in use. The owners occupied a spacious suite with a full bath, designated Room 1, on the first floor, just down the hall from the kitchen, dining hall and lobby. Room 2, the presidential suite, was currently vacant and generally reserved for family members or visiting dignitaries when school was in session.

When I registered, the owners told me they liked to assign the rooms from the top down. I suspected part of the top-down rationale was to maximize the noise buffer between their floor and the guests'. Whatever the reason, I was assigned Room 8 on the third floor in a building without air conditioning. The room adjacent to mine, number 7, was also recently occupied, I was told, although I had not yet had the pleasure of meeting my floormate.

The second brochure I picked up offered an entertaining summary with an insightful overview of Cross Point's number one tourist attraction, Buckland State College. Formed in 1946 with the endowment of a wealthy coal-mining industrialist named Henry Randall and his wife Gwendolyn, BSC was established specifically to educate returning WWII veterans through the GI Bill and to train future educators for the anticipated "baby boom."

Conveniently, the inside panel of the colorfully embossed brochure folded out to a bedsheet-sized illustrated aerial map of the BSC campus, complete with names and annotated descriptions of the buildings. The schematic showed how the campus was laid out like an elaborate maze, spiraling out in concentric squares from the two central buildings at the heart of the plaza. Apparently as new buildings were added, each was designed to save costs by using whatever construction material was available at the time and placed perpendicularly to the previous or nearest building, to keep the maze effect going. It was an amazing architectural achievement, best appreciated from above.

Approximately forty-six hundred students were currently enrolled on the fifty-two-acre campus, with its eighteen multipurpose education buildings, two huge parking lots and a manmade recreational lake. A nineteenth building, a new security facility tentatively named Tanner Hall, was under construction near the south entrance parking lot.

I circled the twin buildings at the center of campus, labeled Randall Hall and Gwendolyn Hall. Side by side, they were the first two buildings constructed in 1946; Randall's clock tower distinguished it from Gwendolyn's bell tower. According to the brochure, Gwendolyn Hall housed administrative offices. That's where tomorrow, after passing through security, I would go to obtain permission to tour the campus. Randall would be my next stop. Not mentioned in the brochure, but covered explicitly all over the internet, Randall Hall's auditorium was where Sonja Olson's corpse was found.

6

I set my alarm for six a.m. but stayed in bed until seven, taking advantage of the crisp spring country air wafting through the open windows, the handstitched patchwork quilt on the bed and the overstuffed down pillows that guaranteed, according to the Happy Orchard Inn brochure, "a peaceful night's sleep for every guest"—to which, I had to admit, my quiet night's slumber was testament.

Alas, when Mother Nature called and I could no longer linger in bed, I stepped into the hallway to find the common bathroom occupied. I put my ear to the door. I could hear the shower. I pounded on the door anyway.

"Hey! How much longer you gonna be?"

When I didn't get an answer, I did what any man in my predicament would do. I walked downstairs to the second-floor bathroom and, finding it unoccupied, stepped inside and relieved my bladder.

With that pressing matter out of the way, I marched back to my room, grabbed my complimentary toothbrush and towel, and returned to the third-floor bathroom, only to find it still occupied.

I pounded on the door. "Hey, what gives? You've been in there long enough. Didn't they tell you this is a communal bathroom?"

I pounded again. Harder.

The door swung open. Steam issued forth in a thick cloud. When it cleared, a scantily clad woman stood in the doorway, wearing a white HOI monogrammed towel wrapped around her head and another tucked around her damp curvy torso. Tiny beads of water glistened on her eyelids while her pale green eyes swept over me languidly and with apparent delight.

"It's all yours," she said, handing me her bar of soap as she slipped past. I watched her sashay down the hall to her room, where she slammed the door closed behind her.

⁕ ⁕ ⁕ ⁕ ⁕ ⁕ ⁕

I'd just finished stuffing the BSC brochure into the breast pocket of my blazer when I heard a gentle rap on my door. I opened it to find the woman from Room 7 standing in the hallway fully dressed. Her strawberry-blonde hair was knotted in a ponytail that reached the middle of her back. She wore makeup, which made her gemlike eyes sparkle all the more. The rest of her came suitably packaged in a loose white blouse and tight black skirt with matching pumps. Whoever said clothes make the man—er, woman—knew exactly what he was talking about. While I might have preferred the terrycloth I saw her in earlier, my imagination lacked for nothing given her present outfit.

"Are you ready?" she gushed with a girl-next-door smile.

"Ready for what?" I managed timidly.

"Breakfast. I'll even let you buy, to make up for your impatience this morning." She glanced down at my left hand. "I see you're not married. I can understand why!"

"I don't know about you, sister, but I've got plans today," I replied with growing annoyance. She seemed to be taking a few things for granted, and that didn't sit well with me at eight o'clock in the morning, especially since I wasn't in the habit of debating about breakfast.

"Mother warned me you might be stubborn, but not stupid."

"What's that supposed to mean? Whose mother?"

"Seriously? I'm Rachel Lynwood. Here to escort you on your grand tour around the BSC campus. That's where you'd be smart to accept."

"What makes you think I need an escort?"

"*She* does. Otherwise, you won't get past security. Plus, I know where the bathrooms are located on campus. Now, if we're done here, I sure could use that cup of coffee."

* * * * * * * *

"Don't you want to know what else Mother said about you?" she asked after we slid into a booth at McKenna's and ordered.

"No."

"Are you always such a bear in the morning, Mac? It is all right if I call you Mac, isn't it?"

"Look, Rachel. I don't mean to seem disrespectful, but why are you here? I work alone. If you looked me up for this case, then you should know that about me."

"Of course I know that about you. Nick gave me the skinny on you. That may work for you in Trenton, but here in Cross Point, you're a fish out of water. I grew up here."

29

"I get that, Rachel. But what is it that you do? Shouldn't you be doing it?"

A young blonde waitress I figured for both a townie and a student brought our breakfasts: a latte and croissant for Rachel and a cup of black coffee with a sticky cinnamon bun for me.

"I'm a journalist. Independent, mostly. But I occasionally write a piece for the *Cross Point Stitch*, the local newspaper—rag that it is. Money is money."

"So you don't live in the area anymore?"

"I travel, mostly."

"How come you're not staying with your mother while you're in town?"

"Seriously, Mac? You've met my mother. Could you stay with her? I lived with her for over thirty years. I think that's enough."

"She seems pleasant enough to me. Just a little obsessed."

"Obsessed? You don't know the half of it!"

"I take it you know all about your mother's unsuccessful first marriage to Ryan Hardwick?"

"Of course. This town has few secrets. I would have found out eventually if she hadn't told me."

"I guess that means you're not in town for the funeral, unless you write obituaries."

"Good riddance. That's where my mother and I are alike."

The waitress came over and dutifully refilled my cup. Rachel passed on another latte. I gave her the benefit of the doubt. Maybe she'd heard about my budgetary shortfall.

"Your mother told me you've tried to get the police records for the Sonja Olson case without any luck. Was that for her, or do you share her suspicions?"

Rachel swirled the creamy remnants of her latte in her cup before setting it back down on the saucer. She glanced around the cozy luncheonette, where the pastel walls were decorated with banners from the various Group III schools that played in the same sports division as BSC. I counted pennants from Albright, Bridgewater, Drew, Emerson, Gettysburg, Kenyon, Montclair, Neumann, and Ursinus, among others. Hanging front and center over the deli counter, none were larger than BSC's inspirational red and black colors: black, symbolic of the anthracite coal that brought Henry Randall his wealth; red, for the Native American ancestry that ran through his wife Gwendolyn's veins. For a brief moment, Rachel's eyes settled at the big café window, as mine settled on her. Then she turned back to our conversation.

"Frankly, I don't know what to believe, Mac. Like I said, Cross Point has few secrets. The Olson murder is certainly one of them. Maybe not the only one, but probably the biggest because it remains unsolved. Unfortunately, the specter of the heinous crime hasn't faded away. With the internet, it seems to be growing larger and weirder every day. That's why you're here: to sort it out for us and put it to rest."

"If I can, Rachel. But it happened such a long time ago. People who were around at that time, people who might have known something, seen something, are long gone."

She considered the thought. "Like Ryan Hardwick, you mean."

"Like Ryan Hardwick and his police chief father, Lionel Hardwick."

"Sheldon Hardwick's still around."

"Sheldon Hardwick?"

"Yeah, Ryan's younger brother."

"Ryan had a younger brother? Did he work in law enforcement, too?"

"No. Apparently he didn't inherit the aptitude. He works at the post office."

7

Despite my earlier misgivings, Rachel Lynwood was slowly growing on me, turning out to be a pleasant surprise and almost delightful company. Buoyant, relaxed, and self-assured, I found her not at all like her aloof and reserved mother. If she was the daughter of a straightlaced old fashionista and a haughty, well-to-do educator, the influence didn't show. Quite the opposite, it seemed. Perhaps it was simply a rebellious streak that she developed to combat her parents' pretentiousness. However, for most children coming from wealth and prestige, the rebellion phase usually lasted through the teen years and maybe into their mid-twenties, not much beyond. Certainly, it would seem out of step for the self-reliant, *single* woman hovering around middle age that I saw before me. That thought was scary and left open a huge question near which I dared not tread, at least not yet.

If spending time with Rachel Lynwood was proving to be tolerable, even fun, it was probably because I had no expectation. In fact, up until we finished breakfast, I kept looking for ways to ditch my newest appendage. Now I found myself looking forward to our guided campus tour.

Like the free spirit she was, Rachel insisted she drive the short distance from the center of town to BSC. I didn't argue. From what I gleaned of her attitude toward life, raising a flag for the cause of chauvinism seemed pointless. So I didn't.

The surprises didn't stop there. She picked me up in a well-maintained cream-colored Karmann Ghia, a two-door German convertible coupe made by Volkswagen that went out of production in 1974. Were the car gods toying with me, or had I just discovered my automotive soul mate?

Only when we were waved straight through security did I realize just how wise the decision had been to let Rachel take the lead. Judging from two things, her rapport with the pimple-faced booth guard and the alumni parking tag hanging from her rearview mirror, I gathered she'd frequented the campus regularly. When the smitten security guard handed her two green visitor passes to hang around our necks without even asking for IDs, my suspicion was confirmed, my curiosity piqued.

"When did you actually go to school here, Rachel?"

"I graduated in '91. Nick was a couple of years ahead of me."

"You ran with an older crowd."

She gave me a sideways glance. "Still do. Like my mother, I suppose. My father was seven years her senior."

We entered through the south gate, the main entrance to the college when coming from the north end of town. Rachel made a left onto Campus Drive, a two-lane access road that ran around the perimeter of the college, ending in a sharp right turn into Parking Lot A at the western edge of the grounds. With only a handful of vehicles visible in the big lot, she had her pick of parking spaces.

She nosed her car up to the sidewalk adjacent to Coleman Hall. The Graphic Arts Building, I noted, pulling the brochure from my pocket to orient myself. Rachel tore it from me and tossed it into the rear of the Karmann Ghia. "You won't be needing that," she said bluntly.

"I like to know where I am," I added defensively.

"You're with me. Does anything else matter?" She hesitated. "Or were you thinking we might get separated?"

I shrugged as I stepped away from the car. "Anything could happen."

She lifted her shoulder bag and hopped out, stopping momentarily to glance up at the darkening sky. A cluster of gray clouds had moved in and begun to hover around what had been, like her mood, a bright morning sun.

"That sky looks ominous," she said, handing me her bag. "At least we don't have far to walk." She put the convertible top up on the Karmann Ghia and locked it in place. She made quick work of it—so quick, I didn't think to offer to help. But then again, maybe that was why she handed me her bag. Like me—until now, at least—she worked well alone. When it came to the top, she had a system. Wouldn't any girl who lived alone and owned a convertible Karmann Ghia?

With the tan top up, the VW resembled a cream puff with chocolate frosting.

"Cute," I said admiringly when she came over to retrieve her bag.

"A real classic, you mean." She deadpanned. "Like the owner."

"You said that, not me."

"Yeah, but that's what you were thinking."

"Stop thinking you know what I'm thinking. It makes me think I'm thinking out loud."

We followed the walkway inward past several buildings like we were skipping along the Yellow Brick Road. Without my handy map, I could not name them until we came upon their respective signs. Most were classrooms for one discipline or another, like Truman Hall of Science and Technology and the Knapp Building of Engineering. According to Rachel, the residence buildings were at the northern and eastern quadrants, not that we'd expect to find a lot of students there. A handful of summer school students were about, strolling along with a group of touring high school students, but not much more human activity was in evidence.

Although laid out like a maze, the concrete walkways had interconnecting routes at specific locations for those who knew where they were going and wanted to get there quicker. That was Rachel. I just followed her lead until we reached the inner sanctum of the central plaza where two identical red brick buildings stood like matching monuments. Gwendolyn Hall, the nearer of the two, was our first destination. That's where we met Chang.

The titular head of the BSC campus security was leaning against the railing, waiting for us on the top step outside the administration building.

"Good morning, Ray," Rachel greeted him warmly. "To what do we owe the pleasure?"

"Cut the shit, Rache. Rose called a half-hour ago. Said you and some investigator were on your way to check out the auditorium." He glanced at me. "Is this the guy?"

"Ray Chang, meet McKenzie Cole."

The muscular Asian American's handshake was no friendlier than his demeanor.

"Rose can be very persuasive," I said cordially, hoping my familiarity with the formidable widow Lynwood might help ease tensions with our uniformed host.

36

"Buddy, you don't know the half of it. She'll tell you," he added, pointing to Rachel. "Her father, Carter Lynwood, was a saint. Revered around here. Best provost BSC ever had ..."

"... and the longest serving," Rachel reminded him.

"Yeah, but her mother is a royal pain in the ass ..."

"... who, unfortunately for Ray, retains close ties with various members of the BSC Board," Rachel finished for him.

He scowled at her, his nostrils flaring slightly as only an Asian's can. I could almost hear Chang thinking, *Spoiled brat. Like mother, like daughter.* At the moment, I was thinking it, too.

If Rachel was bemused by Chang's stare, she didn't show it. Perhaps they'd been through this kind of bantering before.

"I'll give you ten minutes," Chang said, turning to me. "Then I've got to get back to Tanner. In case you haven't heard, we've got a new office building going up."

Thankfully, Randall Hall with its auditorium was only fifty yards away. The three of us walked there in silence with Chang a step or two ahead of us, but not nearly fast enough for his liking, I'm sure.

He had a huge set of keys dangling from his uniform belt like a jailer in an old western movie. When we reached the front entrance of the red brick building, he selected a large brass key with a blotch of red paint on it and unlocked the heavy wooden double doors.

Inside, the air was heavy and musty. It smelled old but not ancient.

"Wait here," he said. Guided by the sunlight streaming in through the open doors, he walked down the hall a few paces until he found the door to the utility room. He

37

inserted another key, stepped inside, and flicked on the bank of lights that illuminated the lower level.

He motioned us forward with a wave of his arm. "This way."

We followed him into the rear of the large auditorium. He flicked on another set of overhead lights, and the rows and aisles leading to the stage lit up. The upholstery was dark and plush and smelled new. "The seats were renovated last year while the school was shut down during the pandemic," he said as if reading our thoughts. Or maybe he just decided to get into the role and play tour guide after all?

As we strolled down the center aisle, he pointed to the stage, where the heavy black curtains were pulled open. He continued his narration as we walked. "The curtains are new, but the floor is original. Been waxed and polished a couple hundred times, but the wood underneath is authentic. You can tell by the wide, dark grain."

When we came to the orchestra pit, he stopped and pointed to a well-worn blonde wood upright piano on the left side of the stage. "The piano's original, too. It's the one she was playing the night she died. No one has had the nerve to move it!"

8

Her name was not spoken. It didn't need to be. We all knew the "she" in Chang's reference was the naked and dead Sonja Olson. That's why we were there, and *this* stage and *that* piano were *the* props in that real-life tragedy. I could feel a collective shudder emanate from our mystified group.

The sudden chirping of Chang's cell phone playing the first few bars of Queen's "Crazy Little Thing Called Love" shattered the solemn, hypnotic moment of our unified reflection.

"Yeah, what is it?" Chang answered, annoyed. He turned his back to us and stepping away. He listened intently for a few seconds, then ended the call.

"I gotta go. One of the inept construction workers put a jackhammer bit through his foot. Gotta fill out the injury report. Don't touch anything. I'll be back in a few minutes."

As soon as Chang left, Rachel jumped up onto the stage. I followed suit, but not nearly as spryly.

"What are you thinking?" I asked.

She gazed out into the empty seats. "It's so surreal to me. I mean, I must have been in this auditorium a dozen times. Bruce Springsteen played here on his way up, although I was too young to see him. So did America, the Kinks, John Gorka and Dan Fogelberg. I saw them, not knowing. Well, knowing, but not really caring what else happened here until now. It's sacred ground, Mac, literally a hallowed hall."

She did a slow, girlish pirouette and landed facing the piano. We walked over to it together. It was just a battered old upright—a spinet, someone else might call it—with deep hidden scars, superficial scratches, and keys worn down from use. How many fingers, before and after Sonja's, have graced those keys, I wondered?

"I can't believe they left this old relic here," I said, trying to appreciate the likelihood after all this time. "Is it in tune?"

Rachel hesitated, then plucked out a single note. It rang out loud and clear from the stage. She played a C chord. That segued into the first few bars of John Lennon's "Imagine." In the emptiness, it resounded. "Sounds right to me," she said.

"What else can you tell me about the incident, Rachel? I haven't had a chance to read any of the news articles yet. Have you?"

"All of them. Many times over. Every anniversary, when the story's reprinted in the *Stitch*, it's repackaged and embellished. It's frightening."

"Then you are obsessed, like your mother."

"Yes, but for different reasons. Her interest is personal. Mine is professional."

"How so?"

"My mother wants to bury some dark demon that has haunted her. As a journalist, I want to write the story. I want to tell Sonja's story to the world—and tell it the right way."

"I see. So, you do have an ulterior motive for shepherding me around today. I shouldn't be flattered; and your mother's concern is obviously secondary."

Rachel didn't answer. She didn't have to. The answer was as plain as the nose on her face or the typewriter she'd have close at hand. "Who offered you the book deal? Random House?" I guessed. Again she ignored me, but her silence was telltale.

"And what do you hope to get out of it, Mac? Nick said you liked a good challenge. That can't be the real reason for your interest, and I'm sure it's not the money. My mother isn't a Rockefeller, and solving this crime after forty-four years is not going to change the world."

"No, but it may change a few simple minds, in this school and in this town."

"So you're a philosopher now? I guess that trumps humble civil servant, if there really is such a thing."

"I share your skepticism about law enforcement, Rachel, and that of your mother, I really do. But I'm gonna need a whole lot more to convince me something's not kosher with this one. So give it to me. Whatcha got?"

Rachel sat down on the wooden piano bench, looking into the footlights. I sat down beside her. It felt nice and cozy, like storytelling time.

"Well, for one thing, the doors here were locked that day. It happened over the Labor Day weekend, before school started, so most students were not on campus yet. Apparently Sonja came back early, and the family she was renting an off-campus room from had not returned home from their vacation. So it appears Sonja may have decided to squat for a night or two in the basement of Randall Hall, where she could while away the hours practicing at the piano."

"How did she get in if the doors were locked?"

"Locked, but not secure. Remember, this was 1977. Door locks could be jimmied, and windows in a building from the 1940s didn't have solid locks or window screens. It was well known back then that Randall Hall's practice rooms downstairs were hangouts that could be breached easily, and frequently were. BSC was an open campus back then. Not like it is today."

"This ease of accessibility could have aided the murderer, too."

"Absolutely."

"When did Ryan Hardwick claim he discovered the body?"

"Around eleven-thirty p.m. According to reports, he was making his usual rounds when he noticed Sonja's bicycle in the bike rack out front."

"He knew it was *her* bike?"

"Apparently. That's how she got around. She didn't have a car on campus. The story goes that she'd spent the summer hitchhiking through Canada and ended up here earlier than expected."

"That's some free-spirited girl."

"Totally. Only you can't really call her a girl, Mac. She was twenty-five going for her master's. Music was her passion. That's all she cared about."

"No boyfriends?"

"None."

"Any enemies?"

Rachel shrugged. "The same with friends. She was pretty much a loner and liked it that way."

"What about her parents? What were they like?"

"Educators, from the liberal 'Sun and Fun State' of California. That's how she came to choose BSC. Her father spent time as a professor at Swarthmore. He died soon after she, in a plane crash. The mother perished in a car accident."

"Are you suggesting the deaths are related?"

"No, just, that's so much tragedy for one family. Fairly open-minded people, from what I've heard. Sonja had a younger sister. Don't know much about her, though."

"Okay, so if Sonja had been crashing here, that might explain why she was found naked, right? Because if she wasn't raped, and it appears she wasn't, then she might have enjoyed practicing in the buff, especially on a hot summer night, alone in an old building without air conditioning."

"Sounds bizarre, I know. But, stranger things have been known to happen. And what else have we got?"

"That's what I don't get, Rachel. What would anyone, Ryan Hardwick in particular, as your mother seems to believe, have against Sonja that would make him want to kill her? What is motive enough to kill someone who comes across as friendless, alone, and aloof; someone who is independent, self-reliant, and engrossed in her music?"

"She was also beautiful, Mac. From the pictures I've seen, she was a real looker. Even you might have been tempted."

"To kiss her, maybe, but to kill her, no way."

"What if she repelled your ardent advances? What if things got out of hand and you lost your temper?"

"Is that what you think happened, Rachel? Some guy got turned down, lost his cool and went apeshit on her, beating her to death with, what ... a baseball bat he just happened to bring along with him?"

"Not just some guy, Mac. Ryan Hardwick, with the butt of his gun, or his nightstick, whatever it was campus cops carried around with them to make them feel macho."

"Listen to yourself, Rachel. He was married at the time. To your mother, no less!"

"And she worked on campus, in the bursar's office. Maybe Sonja threatened to spill the beans."

"Would Ryan risk that, after just a few months of marriage?"

"I don't know, Mac. You're a guy. Would you?"

"There's a bit of particularly sage advice in a situation like that. Maybe you've heard it. Goes, 'You don't shit where you eat.'"

"Of course, but that doesn't stop everyone."

"No, it doesn't. I'll be the first to admit weak men can buckle for any number of reasons, and lust knows no bounds once ignited. But I still have a hard time believing, despite any bedroom eccentricities, that a newly married, newly hired BSC security guard, whose father was chief of police in town—and, let's not forget, the guy who reported the crime in the first place—would commit the heinous crime of passion seemingly orchestrated here."

Rachel seemed to chew on the "bedroom eccentricities" remark but chose not to comment. Did she know? Did her mother tell her that part of the story?

"I hear you, Mac, and I would have grave doubts myself, were it not for the psychic's remarks, which have been totally cast aside."

"Psychic? The police brought in the services of a psychic?"

"No. Just some random psychic who lived in the community offered his insights. I can't seem to recall his name. No one took him seriously, though."

"What did he say?"

Rachel spun around on the stool, stood, and threw her hands down on the piano keys with such force that the piano leg to my left wobbled. I leaned my knee against it to make it stop.

"He stood right here, just like this, and claimed he could see the whole thing happening like a movie. He saw a man in a uniform, with a ring of keys dangling from his belt, standing over Sonja Olson and beating her naked body with a wooden stick or pole."

"Did he see a face?"

"No."

"How about an insignia on the uniform, or the color?"

"No identifiable symbols. The uniform was dark in color. Some have taken that to be a maintenance uniform, or possibly ..."

"Hey!" shouted Ray Chang, clapping his hands to get our attention, causing his keys to shake and jangle as he strolled down the center aisle. "I told you two not to touch anything. Time to go. Chop, chop."

"... a security guard," Rachel finished in a hushed whisper.

9

The rain had started while we were in the auditorium, attempting to reconstruct the unfavorable past many would have preferred remain buried and forgotten. A typical spring downpour, it didn't quite qualify as "raining cats and dogs," but it was sudden and brief. It must have been raining, or threatening to, when Chang returned to Randall Hall from the construction site, because he arrived in one of the campus security vehicles, a modified electric golf cart with a canopy top. He offered us a ride back to our car but nowhere else.

"How's the construction worker?" Rachel inquired, making conversation ... or so I thought.

"He'll live," replied Chang coldly. "The contractor will contact ICE. He'll get sent back to Mexico or wherever. They'll replace him with another wetback and the work will go on like nothing happened."

"What happens to your injury report?" I asked.

"Who knows? The insurance company's not likely to see it, though."

Rachel squirmed in her seat. "Doesn't that bother you?"

"It's not my problem. My job is to fill out the accident report so the school's protected if the shit hits the fan.

Where it goes after I turn in my report is beyond my pay grade."

"I'd say we're done here," she sighed from the back seat.

∗ ∘ ❀ ❀ ∘ ∗

"Planning to write a tell-all?" I asked Rachel after we climbed into her car.

"Yeah, I can see the real Pulitzer potential in exposing an illegal immigration ring operating at a publicly funded state school construction site. I'll be the toast of the town."

I saw her point. "More likely you'll get toasted."

"Exactly. I think I'll stick to a forty-four-year-old murder mystery. Not quite as controversial."

She started the car and switched on the windshield wipers, clearing away the pitter-pattering raindrops.

"You see what you're up against, here, don't you?" she said, turning toward me. There was obvious concern etched in her normally cheerful, confident face.

"I see it. Not exactly open arms. But I didn't expect it would be. Nobody likes it when some outsider comes snooping around where he's not wanted."

"Ready to call it a day, then?"

"Hell no, I'm just getting started," I replied stubbornly. I seemed to be the least informed guy in town. I needed a crash course, pronto. "Time for me to get up to speed on what everybody else in this damn place seems to know already about the Olson case."

"How do you plan to do that?"

"Ordinarily, I'd march over to the police station and demand answers. But we both know that's not gonna work. I'll just have to wait and see if my Plan B opens things up for me."

Rachel grinned. She was impressed that I had a Plan B. She also thought she knew what else was coming.

"In the meantime, I could continue to pick your brain until I know at least what you know."

"But, you're not going to do that?"

"Nope."

"Because you think it will be too subjective?"

"Because that's not how I work. It's not enough. Your mother hired *me*, not you."

"Okay, so where do we go from here?"

"How's the Lewis Library sound to you?"

"Dated."

"Naturally. Coming from me, what did you expect?"

"Do you really want me to comment on that?"

"No, but how about if you run me over to the library anyway. If I recall correctly, it's on the east side of campus. You can take Campus Drive to get there."

"And what am I supposed to do while you're 'getting up to speed'?"

"That's up to you. You're the one who volunteered to play tour guide."

"I'll tell you what," said Rachel, reaching inside her shoulder bag. "Give me your hand."

"Why?"

She made a doleful face. "Well, I'm not going to arm wrestle you."

I held out my left hand. Using a Sharpie marker she had pulled from her bag, she proceeded to write two cryptic words on my open palm: *Rach3* and *W00dyL*.

"What do they mean?"

"They're my User ID and Password."

"For what?"

49

She reached down into her bag again and withdrew her iPad. No wonder the bag felt so weighted before. "For this. Everything you need to know about the Olson case, you can find using the tablet and accessing the internet. It'll save you a ton of time. You can use it in the library if you want, or I can take you back to the Inn."

"What are you going to do?"

"I'm going to get my nails done, so when we meet for dinner later, you'll marvel at how nice they look reflected in my shimmering glass of Chateau Ste. Michelle Sauvignon Blanc."

"Where's dinner?"

"The Whispering Pines Tavern."

"That redneck lodge, next to the Happy Orchard Inn?"

"Looks can be deceiving. Look at you."

"Point made. What time?"

"Seven p.m."

"How am I supposed to get back to town if I go to the library?"

"There's a shuttle bus that leaves every hour from BSC. You can pick it up in front of the library. It will drop you off at the post office across from the Inn.

"Take this." She handed me a card with her photo encased in plastic, displaying the BSC seal. "This is my alumni card. Free BSC Shuttle service is one of the perks. Don't lose it."

"It's got your picture on it."

"Put your thumb over it. Don't you know anything?"

I rolled down the window. The rain had stopped. Perfect time for an adventurous walk around the campus for atmosphere and mood.

"Any other questions?"

I reached behind her. "Mind if I take my brochure with me? I think I'll walk."

⁕ ⁕ ⁕ ⁕ ⁕ ⁕ ⁕ ⁕

I spent the better part of Thursday afternoon sitting in one of those private cubicles on the second floor of the Lewis Library. No one bothered me for hours because basically no one was there. But for a handful of library staffers, I was the only patron on the premises. I was sure that was not the case when school was in session. I hoped not. Had we reached the point where the digital world had replaced the need for library books for good?

I, for one, missed the smell of aging leather. When working in my office, I kept a few classics on hand, just for the aesthetic. It harkened back to my own college days and always put me in a studious mood. So, even though I was using Rachel's iPad linked to the internet for the Olson research, I found myself comforted by the antiquity of my surroundings, even if I wasn't consulting the knowledge tucked behind the old musty bindings.

By four p.m., I was satisfied I had devoured every news article, blog entry, and chatroom opinion offered online about the Olson case through the decades. Surprisingly, nearly all of what I read confirmed or supported what the Lynwood women had separately shared with me. Maybe I shouldn't have been surprised at all. There was no basis for deception or gaps in the recollections from either.

The few nuggets of new information I could scrounge up did not amount to much. But they did leave open certain doors I was hoping the actual police reports would either open wider or close permanently for me.

For example, I learned the victim's face had been beaten beyond recognition. As a result, Sonja's corpse came to be identified by one of her professors by the cut and color of her hair. Multiple students told police that Sonja supposedly had a boyfriend, a local fireman, but his name never surfaced in the press. Since no arrest was ever mentioned in any of the papers, it was either a false lead or he had an airtight alibi. Of course it was possible the boyfriend slipped through the police dragnet, such that it was. That question might get answered more fully when TPD Chief Perkins comes through with copies of the actual police reports.

Additionally, as I found interesting, the Randall Hall auditorium was in use over that holiday weekend before the start of school. It played host to the Cross Point Players, a community-based theater troupe that had performed a version of the Broadway musical "Hair" onstage the night before. Evidently, the cast and crew had completely vacated the premises at least twenty-four hours earlier.

I also learned the name of the supposed psychic Rachel had alluded to earlier. He was a local-yokel named Johnson Sinclair. Although I doubted I would still find him alive or living in the area, I made a note to see if I could locate him for an interview.

10

What Rachel had neglected to tell me about her nail appointment was that it was made for her and her mother prior to our morning tour of BSC.

While at Flo's Crow Nest, as the beauty shop was amusingly referred to by BSC students, mother and daughter took the opportunity to update one another.

"How are things coming along with our favorite new PI?" Rose Lynwood asked as Florence Sweeney, the shop's hip proprietor and namesake, took an emery board to her nails.

"I'm still a little surprised you agreed to hire him in the first place," replied Rachel, sitting next to her. "I didn't think he would appeal to you. He's not your type. A bit unpolished."

"Such things can be overlooked when confronted with a challenging mind," she said sagely. "And you?"

"I find his rough edges attractive. He doesn't come across as the hardheaded Neanderthal or heavy-handed misogynist that I had expected."

"My, we are complimentary today. Could it be you're very taken with him?"

"Jury's still out. We're having dinner tonight at Whistling Pines."

The manicurist smiled to herself. This was big news around Cross Point. She was getting it firsthand and couldn't wait to repeat it.

"That should be fun. Has he been helpful?" Rose asked. "With the book?"

"You've been honest with him about that?"

"He has the right to know where my interests lie on the subject. I wish I could say the same for you, Mother."

"Whatever do you mean, dear?"

"For decades, while Dad was alive, Ryan Hardwick was *persona non grata* and any discussion about the Olson murder was taboo. Now suddenly you're willing to pay someone to get to the bottom of both mysteries."

Flo Sweeney dropped her emery board on the floor. She cursed as she got up to fetch a sterile replacement from the counter and return quickly so she wouldn't miss a word. Unfortunately for her, the shop telephone rang and she hurried off to answer it. Customers were not all that plentiful when school was not in session.

Mother and daughter shared a knowing smile, watching Flo's antics before returning to their now completely private conversation.

"They're one and the same," admitted Rose.

"Only you believe that, Mother. But what does it matter? He's dead now, and you haven't had anything to do with him in forty-four years."

"I can't tell you why, but it's important to me."

"You're obsessed. Why can't you just let the dead rest in peace?"

"You seem more upset than usual when we talk about this, sweetie. What's changed?"

"What if nothing's changed? What if Mac fails like everybody else has? What if he comes up emptyhanded? What then?"

"I understand your apprehension, dear. We have nothing but threads to go on, and time is definitely against us. We've got to hope McKenzie Cole comes through. He's our best hope, if he can get his hands on the official reports. I believe they hold the key to everything."

◦ ◦ ◦ ◉ ◉ ◦ ◦

At around six p.m. it started raining again, a warm misty drizzle, as I stood inside the bus shelter in front of the Lewis Library waiting for the BSC shuttle. The red and black van came right on time. I reasoned the short ride back to town would get me to the hotel in time for a quick shower and a change of clothes before my scheduled dinner date at the tavern next door with Rachel.

I should have known better. Within minutes of taking a seat, my cell phone rang. I was expecting Rachel but then realized we hadn't exchanged phone numbers. To my surprise it was my secretary calling from the office. Score another late night for the indefatigable Mary Porter.

"Hi, Mary. Don't you ever go home?"

"Hello, Mac. I thought I might hear from you earlier. Everything okay up there?"

"Just dandy. A little rainy right now, but I'm about to drink some of the dampness away."

There was a long pause on Mary's end. "Oh, were you planning to stay another night at the Inn?"

"Can we afford it?"

"We can it afford, Mac. It's just that Chief Perkins called earlier. He said to tell you it was very important for you to get down to the station first thing tomorrow morning. He's got what you asked for, but it has to be returned by the end of the day. 'It's now or never.' His words, not mine. You've got one shot at it."

"That's terrific news, Mary," and I meant it. It was indeed very exciting news, sooner and less of a hassle than I expected. Bill Perkins knew how to pull the right strings. He certainly had a charming way about him and was a consummate professional. When he said "go," you did not hesitate.

Although I was looking forward to an engaging dinner and drinks with the ever-delightful Rachel Lynwood, I knew I'd have to put my ardor on hold, put the cork in the bottle, and get back to Trenton right away so I'd be fresh as a daisy in the morning. Work before pleasure. Always. That's my motto.

"Mac? You still there?"

"Yeah, Mary, but I won't be for long. I'm on my way back to the Inn as we speak. I'm going to ask them to hold the room for me just in case I need to get back here tomorrow."

"Is it wise to spend money on lodging when you don't know where you will be?"

"It's not exactly the frugal thing to do, Mary, I agree. But good rooms are hard to come by up here in the sticks, and this one rocks. I slept like a baby last night. And I still have plenty of work left to do here."

I could sense Mary calculating the costs in her head and reading between the lines simultaneously, but she was smart enough to ignore the elephant in the room.

"If you say so, Mac. But you still have some things pending down here that need your attention."

"Leave them on my desk. I'll swing by the office and attend to them after I'm finished down at the station."

"Drive safely, Mac. Watch out for deer. The four-legged kind, and the other."

Mary hung up, having had the final word, as always. Usually it was a cautionary one about my two insatiable appetites: Jack Daniels and dames. I swear, Mary Porter could smell my urges a mile away. That's probably why I've kept her on all these years. Besides being an excellent secretary, she often doubled as my personal vice enforcer … for minimum wage!

The shuttle let me off at the Cross Point Post Office, another destination on my list of local attractions to see, but not tonight. The post office was closed, so a visit to the younger Hardwick at his place of employment would have to wait until another day.

Entering the Inn, my primary concerns were changing clothes, re-renting my lovely room through the weekend, and getting a hold of Rachel Lynwood in order to reschedule our dinner date. The beak-nosed, bird-faced owner of the inn, Mark Abrams, appeared behind the hotel desk when I entered the lobby.

"There you are!" he said flamboyantly. "I was beginning to wonder what to do with your luggage."

"You're welcome to keep it for the weekend if there's a vacancy in Room 8," I said, knowing there would be this time of year, even though I had led Mary to believe otherwise.

"A pleasure," Abrams replied giddily. He passed the register over to me to sign. I inked my John Hancock illegibly, as I always did when it came to trivial legal matters, then flipped to the blank last page, tore it out, and scribbled a note:

> *My apologies. Pressing work in Trenton;*
> *TPD has docs. Must review ASAP or forfeit*
> *peek. Leaving NOW! Save appetite(s) and*
> *hold the fort... Mac*

I folded the note and handed it to Mark, along with Rachel's iPad. "Would you see that Room 7 gets these the minute I'm gone?" In an instant, the hotel manager's facial expression changed from dour to conspiratorial. I checked my pocket for my car keys. Nothing remained in my room that couldn't stay, including a change of clothes. Then I made a mad dash in the rain for the parking lot, all the while congratulating myself for having had the foresight to put my top up when I arrived yesterday.

11

I got to police headquarters on North Clinton Avenue late but a few steps ahead of Chief Perkins. After a leisurely but rainy and fog-filled ride home through the Pennsylvania countryside the night before, I found the shock of waking up to an alarm clock back in Trenton a painful adjustment. At the Happy Orchard Inn, it was nice to get up whenever I got up, instead of when some pressing matter forced me awake at a specific time.

The police station was already humming with activity, as drunks and prostitutes held in cells overnight were being released on bail bonds posted by early-to-rise attorneys and night-owl pimps. The more criminally inclined prisoners were being processed for transfer to county sheriff's officers, while a new shift of yawning uniformed men and women—to-go cups in hand—shuffled in and out of the building.

Perkins greeted everyone warmly, then ushered me into the small tactical conference room where, much to my chagrin, Detective Greg O'Malley was already seated and poring over a stack of papers.

The room was cold and windowless but functional. It had a central oval table with six chairs around it. A mobile blackboard took up most of the space in the front of the room. A stainless-steel coffee urn and a gurgling water cooler occupied a small countertop in the rear. A half-dozen lidded file boxes were piled high on carts, as the plump and cheerful Shirley Mae Brown wheeled in another.

"That's the last of them, Chief," she said, throwing a flirtatious wink my way before easing herself out the door.

"I asked O'Malley to join us," said Perkins, reading the disgruntled look on my face. "He's in between cases at the moment, and I thought you could use a hand. There's a ton of material to go over and, as you can see, he's gotten a head start."

"Seems like old times, hey, Cole?" quipped O'Malley. "TPD doing your work for you, *again*."

Eager to show my gratitude to Chief Perkins for going out on a limb, I struggled to keep my hostility toward O'Malley in check.

"The hand, I could use, thank you," I replied cordially enough. "The sarcasm, I can do without."

"Play nice, fellas," chided Perkins. "Otherwise we'll be in for a very long day."

Perkins closed the conference room door. I chose the chair at the opposite end of the table from O'Malley. Perkins sat between us. O'Malley chuckled as he loosened his tie. Clearly he was enjoying himself at my expense. His salt-and-pepper hair was neatly brushed back, and his lifeless gray eyes hung wide open, no doubt from too much caffeine. He checked his coffee cup. It was empty.

"What's so funny?" I asked between clenched teeth.

"I don't know what the deal is here, Cole, but if you're looking for police impropriety, you're barking up the wrong tree."

"When I want your opinion, I'll give it to you," I said angrily. This was not going well, and we hadn't even started. Between us there was a lot of history that kept us barely civil at times.

I gave Perkins a stern look. "You told him?"

"I had to tell him something so he had something to look for. You didn't exactly give us much to go on, Mac."

"Needle in a haystack," opined O'Malley. "Unless your client is trying to discredit the CPPD for something that happened some forty years ago."

"What brought you to that conclusion, detective?" inquired Perkins with genuine interest.

O'Malley pushed a packet of papers toward Perkins. "It's all here. It's thorough and exhaustive. Three hundred interviews. Cross Point Police, BSC Campus Security, and the FBI conducted over three hundred interviews back in 1977, including statements from students, faculty, administrators, and members of the community. They turned up bupkis."

"Have you read all the statements?" I asked.

"No, but I don't think we need to. The summary highlights the bulk of them, and they all say pretty much the same thing. The victim was a recluse. Apparently, she had little interaction with anyone on or off campus. No enemies and no friends."

"Well, someone knew her," I argued, "and he got to her."

"A stranger, maybe. Someone totally random in a random act."

"Making it likely untraceable," sighed Perkins.

"What about the boyfriend, the local fireman?" I asked.

"Speculation, without substance," replied O'Malley. "A red herring, maybe."

"If so, planting it would suggest intention on someone's part," noted Perkins. "Possible premeditation as well."

"I need to read this stuff for myself," I said. "That's the only way I can be sure."

Perkins pushed the packet of paper my way. A manila folder lay on top.

"What's this?" I inquired.

"Photographs," replied O'Malley. "Brace yourself. You're not going to like what you see."

He was right. None of the news articles I read contained any photos of the victim taken at the crime scene, and for good reason. They were utterly gruesome and horrifying. The pictures painted thousands of words, worse than any description of the corpse in any of the news reports.

I handed the photo folder to Perkins. "What do these prints say to you about the killer, Chief?"

Perkins scanned them one at a time. When he finished, he spread them all out on the table for the three of us to admire. Blood was everywhere: pooled on the floor, spattered on the sheet music, running down a piano leg, dripping from the keys, and oozing through the white piano cover that lay bunched in the corner. The victim's face was a pile of bloody pulp under a clump of close-cropped blonde hair.

Perkins tapped Sonja Olson's high school senior photo that was released to the media. "Such a beautiful girl. What a nasty way to go. I'd say the perp was pissed. He didn't just want her dead. He wanted her erased and forgotten. If random, it's senseless. If a crime of passion, it's the act of sick mind."

"A sociopath," proffered O'Malley, and I found myself uncharacteristically agreeing with him. "Someone strong and full of uncontrollable rage," he added.

"Police do nothing good for themselves or the community at large by protecting someone like this," Perkins postulated. "If we know, even if we only suspect, we need to get a guy like this off the streets."

"Even if he's one of your own?"

Perkins slammed his fist down on the table. "Especially if he's one of our own. They're the ones who think they can get away with it again."

"He's right, Cole," agreed O'Malley. "A butcher like this has no place in society. He ain't human."

O'Malley felt determined to push the point further. "Could drugs have played a role? Some random student strung out on drugs, who lost it? In that case, Sonja Olson was simply in the wrong place at the wrong time."

"I can't buy into the random theory, O'Malley."

"Me either," O'Malley agreed.

"Why?" asked Perkins.

"Because she was at Randall Hall by choice. Against the rules, maybe, but she was there during that time," I answered for the room. "People knew it. People saw her there. She was *expected* to be there and, so it would seem, to be alone and vulnerable."

"Go on," urged Perkins.

"Because she was found naked and bound …"

"But not sexually assaulted," O'Malley added. "At least not according to these official reports. That's not something forensics can cover up."

"Not now. But how about in 1977, when perpetrated by one of their own?"

"You're reaching, Mac," Perkins cautioned. "That would make it one hell of a coverup, involving dozens of people from several law enforcement agencies."

"Two of the three departments could have been controlled by the same family or group," I argued.

Perkins was adamant. "Not good enough. That leaves the FBI. An agency known for its independence."

"Says who? There are plenty of agents guilty of perversion. It's like a disease that spreads."

"Careful, Mac," Perkins warned. "Let's not cast aspersions without proof ..."

"Or pick fights I can't win," I added for my own benefit.

O'Malley stood and stretched. "I need a break."

"You need a cigarette," I goaded him. There was no use pretending. We all knew he lacked the discipline and the desire to quit. My animosity toward O'Malley stemmed from experience, due mainly to his lack of initiative, his inflated ego and overconfidence. He was a decent detective, just unaware of his own shortcomings, or unconcerned about them. Because, as a TPD lifer, he didn't have to care. Maybe it was a personality flaw. More likely, it was the result of spending an entire career in the toxic city environment.

"Listen, Cole, it comes down to this. After forty-four years, you have no witnesses, no weapon, no motive, and no suspects. In short, no evidence. Ergo, no case."

"I still would like to go over everything myself."

O'Malley reached for the door. "Yeah, yeah, I know. Suit yourself. That's what you get paid to do. But I don't. To me it's a huge waste of time."

Suddenly he stopped. He walked over to one of the carts, tore the lid off a box and rifled through its contents. He pulled out a thick, tabbed beige folder and slid it across the table to me.

"Here's a final thought for you, Cole. Free advice. No charge. You can buy me a drink at Jake's sometime."

"That'll be the day," I mumbled.

"If you're hellbent on reading everything, I suggest you start with the statements taken by the authorities from the theater group. There's a sheet in there with the complete list. Fifty-some-odd people—'odd' being the key word. Actors, stagehands, and crew, all from the community with no known ties to the school. All of them claim to have seen the victim for the last time in Randall Hall the night before she died, and at other times during rehearsals."

"Get to the point," I encouraged him. The clock was ticking.

"In my opinion, the killer is one of them. Think about it. He has no loyalty to the school and no allegiance to the student body. He's someone with an ax to grind, or he's an artist-type, given to wild mood swings. He's now totally unhinged; turned on by the audacity of the play. He's pumping with performance adrenaline and looking to channel his emotions, frustrations, and anxieties. And there she is: a sweet, innocent, beautiful nobody, that nobody will miss!"

◦ ◦ ◉ ◉ ◉ ◦ ◦

I thanked O'Malley for his professional "opinion" and let him shuffle off to fill his aging lungs with carcinogens. (Hey, if he wanted to die a horrible death, why should I try to stop him?) While he was gone, I thought about Sonja Olson. O'Malley's "nobody." Hers really was a horrible death she didn't deserve. I think she would have gladly traded places with O'Malley given the alternative.

At first. I didn't put much stock in O'Malley's theory. I was too annoyed with his arrogance. But Chief Perkins did, and he suggested I give it serious consideration. I agreed to do so, but while Perkins read through the student statements looking for the proverbial "needle in the haystack" that might provide motive, means, and opportunity for someone to execute such a dreadful crime, I picked up the police narrative and found little I didn't already know. Was that all there was? Did the CPPD send us everything, or were they holding something back, I wondered.

O'Malley never returned. An hour later, Shirley Mae came in to tell us O'Malley got waylaid with a new assignment, a suicide downtown near the train station. *How ironic*, I thought. One life senselessly snuffed out, the other awash in self-pity and ended willingly. I moved on to the actors' statements grudgingly.

Around noon, Chief Perkins got called away to a luncheon meeting with the mayor. I poured myself another cup of burnt coffee and thought about O'Malley's theory again. In a way it made sense, for the reasons he cited. I re-scanned the list of Cross Point Players and Crew from the 1977 production of "Hair" to see how many of the fifty-five-or-so statements remained to be read.

Suddenly a bell rang in my head. I jumped out of my chair, nearly spilling the sludge in my cup. Had Shirley Mae been in the room, I would have bear-hugged her, or let her squeeze "the Dickens" out of me.

There, on the second sheet, two-thirds down the page, was a name I recognized. It was a name I'd stumbled upon yesterday, related to the case but in a different context. The list in front of me named Johnson Sinclair as a multitalented twenty-six-year-old with minor acting credits. According to the playbill, this Johnson Sinclair was the understudy for the lead role of Claude as well as a member of the chorus. The Johnson Sinclair I had read about online yesterday was a self-proclaimed psychic who said "a man in a uniform with a ring of keys attached to his belt" was Sonja Olson's murderer. Could they be the same person?

If so, the psychic's scenario was not given to the police in his initial statement. It only surfaced later, through the media. The story grew legs and gave rise to a conspiracy theory about a killer cop and a coverup. At least now I had some support for my client's suspicions about the Ryan Hardwick angle, beyond what went on in their bedroom. The question before me now: Was the paranormal story real or a total fabrication?

I hated the idea that O'Malley might be right—that the killer was a member of the theater group that had performed in Randall Hall the night before. That would make O'Malley see himself as near-prescient (which I couldn't accept), making it much harder to work with him in the future. I consoled myself with the notion that even fools get lucky sometimes.

But when added to the psychic scenario, this name thing was a new and potentially important revelation. What were the chances that someone who saw her nightly from afar also "saw" her stunning murder in a vision he later shared with the world? Johnson Sinclair the psychic and Johnson Sinclair the actor had to be the same person. The name simply wasn't that common, unless they were father and son.

I made quick work of the rest of the statements, reports, and documents, but my mind fixated on the "coincidence." O'Malley's theory was gaining traction with me; it had to be someone from the theater group. Sinclair's age was right, twenty-six. Sonja was twenty-five.

Also tucked away in Sinclair's bio was the little-known fact that he had graduated from Beaver College, BSC's cross-state rival. Coupled with O'Malley's idea, that a performance artist could turn killer when fueled by adrenaline and resentment over not being cast as the primary lead, a pretty strong motive was taking shape— one that could be further developed in a court of law.

What better way to deflect suspicion from your own deplorable actions than by sowing doubt and directing it—post-Watergate—toward the secretive and biased American criminal justice system?

I returned the files to their respective folders, closed the open boxes, and trashed my coffee cup. I gave the photos one last look, cementing my resolve to obtain justice for Sonja and bring this horrible case to an honorable close.

I buzzed Shirley Mae on the intercom and told her to thank Detective O'Malley and Chief Perkins for their invaluable assistance. I believed I had what I needed.

Outside, I paused to let the sun warm my face. Then I dialed my office. The ever-efficient Mary Porter answered on the first ring.

"How's it going, Mac?"

"I'm finished here, Mary."

"Did you find what you were looking for?"

"That may depend on you."

"Me? What can I do?"

"I need you to find someone for me. An address, a phone number, anything you can turn up. His name is Johnson Sinclair."

"Could he be dead?"

"Very likely. If he *is* still alive, he'd be 70 or 71 and possibly living in the Cross Point, Pennsylvania area.

"Occupation?"

"Probably retired, except actors and psychics tend to lead multiple lives. So check for a website or some kind of internet presence."

"Got it. Anything else?"

"Yeah, have those papers ready for me to sign. I'm on my way to the office."

"That reminds me—you did have a call earlier. She was very insistent."

"She?"

"Yes, she claimed to be your current client."

"Rose Lynwood? What did she want?"

"That's not the name she gave. And she didn't sound like the senior citizen you described to me."

"What name did she give, and what did she want?"

"She said her name was Rachel Lynwood, and she wanted your cell number."

"Did you give it to her?"

"Absolutely not."

"Why not?"

"I figured if you hadn't given it to her, why should I? Who is she, Mac?"

"She's our client's daughter."

"Is she our client, too, then?"

"I'm not really sure how to answer that."

"I thought so. Doesn't her mother have your cell number, Mac?"

"What are you getting at, Mary?"

"I gave Rachel Lynwood *my* cell number in case she needed to reach you in an emergency. I told her to pass it along to her mother."

"Now why didn't I think of that? I'll see you shortly."

"No, you won't. It's Friday night. I'm meeting my sister for dinner at Maxine's. It's her turn to buy."

"What about Johnson Sinclair?"

"I'll text you whatever I find."

12

I left the letters and papers stacked and signed on Mary's desk for Monday morning, though I knew she'd be in before then. Spring Saturdays were gardening days for Mary. She really enjoyed getting her hands in the dirt. But what she loved even more was the bounty that resulted from her labors and Nature's blessings—and of course the praise from her boss.

Mary was right about one thing: It was Friday night, and, since I was back in Trenton, that meant a night at my favorite blues haunt, Jake's Joint on Warren and South Broad. Tonight's lineup, I'd been informed, included the area return of Highway 41, a rocking Allman Brothers tribute band that featured my old boyhood chum, Mark "Dickey Betts" Cusato and local legend Ernie "Duane Allman" White on dueling guitars. "Statesboro Blues" was blasting from the stage as I made my way over to the bar. Nick Falcone, Jake's genial mixologist, spied me among the crowd. He had a Jack Daniels on the rocks and a broad grin waiting for me as I slunk into my usual seat at the bar.

"Hey, Partner. Miss me?" I said.

"Like jock rot. Where ya been?"

Dave Hart

"Up in your old neck of the woods. BSC."

The look of bemusement on Nick's handsome face was priceless. "She didn't. She contacted you?"

"She did."

"When?"

"Wednesday."

"Have you met her? Or her mother?"

I nodded. "Quite a pair. But not a matched set," I qualified.

"Don't be so sure." Nick busied himself by wiping down the bar top for show, but, as always, he was curious about my work. "Can you talk about the case?"

I took a slow pull, then put my glass down. "It goes back a ways."

"How far?"

"You were in diapers. 1977."

"Oh! The Olson murder?" Shock registered on his face.

I put up my hands. "You didn't hear it from me."

Nick shook his head, bewildered. "People are still interested in that nightmare?"

"More than ever. It's gained mythical status."

"Because of the internet. I'm not surprised. What's Rachel's interest in it?"

"A possible book deal."

"Hey, if it lands a six-figure advance, I want back in."

"Talk to her."

I took another swig of Jack. "What can you tell me about Rose?"

"A real sweetheart, a gem. She loved me."

"And Carter, the old man?"

"A jackass. A real stuffed shirt. I could never see him with Rose, let alone as Rachel's father."

I could always count on Nick to be candid. Night after night, the bar trade hardened him. He was nothing if not direct with me, but maybe not as much with women.

"I take it the feeling was mutual?"

"The old man threw me out of the house a hundred times."

"Not good enough for his daughter?"

Nick let out a hearty laugh. "I think he worried more about his wife when I was around."

"You snake!"

"Hey, it wasn't me. I just knew how to make her laugh."

"And Rachel?"

"Ah, Mac, she broke my heart. I understand it now. She had to get away from there."

"That bad, huh? Too bad to stay with her own mother when she comes back to town?"

"Yeah, that bad. I don't know what's behind it. I thought it might improve once Carter passed away."

I took another slow sip and changed the subject. "What can you tell me about old man Hardwick?"

"The police chief? He reminded me of Stalin. Clamped down on everything in that town, especially where the college was concerned."

The glass belonging to the guy on the stool next to me ran dry. He glanced up at Nick dejectedly. Nick poured him another Blue Moon draft in a fresh glass, added an orange wedge, and slid him a shot of Jägermeister for good measure.

"How about the sons? Did you know them?"

"They used to hang out at the Whispering Pines Tavern, shooting pool, hustling college kids, and picking up chicks."

I smiled. "Sounds like your kind of crowd."

"Not really. The oldest, Ryan I think his name was, was a chip off the old block. He liked to throw his daddy's name around town."

"And the younger one?"

"He was creepy, spooky, scary!"

"In what way?"

Nick leaned in close. "You know the phrase 'going postal'?" he whispered. "That's him."

"Because he works for the Postal Service?"

"Because he's like Vesuvius—always ready to erupt!"

"Has that ever happened?"

Nick shrugged. "Not that I know of. But I steered clear of him just the same."

"In that case, I can't wait to me him," I said, downing what was left of my reliable liquid balm. I didn't have to ask Nick for a refill.

13

"Saints be praised!" That was my response to Mary's text the following morning after she sent me the info. Mary found a location for a Johnson Sinclair, *Seer Extraordinaire*, and he was not six feet under. He was on the internet and lived about an hour outside of Cross Point, in the foothills of the Alleghenies, just below Blue Mountain.

I gassed up the Jaguar and headed across the Delaware River into Pennsylvania for the long, meandering drive up near the Water Gap. I tried phoning this Johnson Sinclair to make sure he was the right guy before I made the long trek north. But he didn't answer. I got his voicemail and left the message that I was on my way.

The GPS route took me east of Cross Point. I was tempted to stop and check on my room, but was wary of losing time, especially if I ran into Rachel Lynwood. I imagined she was still staying at the Inn, but maybe that was wishful thinking.

I could see Blue Mountain looming, larger with every mile I traveled. Wispy white clouds cloaked its peak. Gradually the highway gave way to narrow rural roads that wended through the foothills and up the mountainside. Vegetation and residences grew sparser until I came to a clearing where a single-story log cabin stood at the end of a long gravel lane. Gray-white smoke billowed from the chimney. A hand-painted sign told me I had arrived at the home/business of Johnson Sinclair, *Seer Extraordinaire.*

I parked the Jag facing the front porch, climbed out of the car, walked up to the door, and knocked. After several minutes, the unpainted wooden door creaked open, as if by an invisible hand. I peered into the darkness. I called out.

"I'm looking for Johnson Sinclair! My name is—"

"I know who you are," came a deep male voice from within. I could see the outline of a sullen face, but the features were indistinguishable.

Did he really know who I was? I wasn't sure if he was just saying it to make a point.

"Then you must know why I'm here," I replied jauntily, hoping to get a rise out of him.

No answer.

How he knew wasn't important. Like Rachel had said, there were few secrets in Cross Point, and I did leave a voicemail. From his curt manner, I knew this Sinclair was not going to make it easy for me. No doubt he saw my appearance after so many years as a nuisance, unwarranted, and a total waste of his time.

"Look, would you mind if I came in and asked you a few questions? I'll keep it brief."

He hesitated, then pulled open the door just enough for me to slip past him and into the house. He surveyed the yard to make sure I was alone, then turned and followed me in, leaving the door slightly ajar—for my escape or his own, I wasn't certain.

Maybe it was to let in a little light, because the house was dark and cool. The anteroom was a séance parlor, separated from the rest of the first floor by a beaded curtain. Smoke curled off the tips of numerous joss sticks on a card table covered with a purple velvet cloth. Two folding chairs flanked it. A solitary block candle, newly lit, provided the only other light in the room.

As my eyes adjusted, I noticed my host had a long, braided gray goatee that hung beneath shallow, sunken cheeks. His eyes were hidden behind red-tinted spectacles. He wore a blue beret, which I presumed covered a bald dome, but somehow a thick silver ponytail hung down his back. He was barefoot and dressed in a peacock blue Nehru jacket with thin black slacks. A huge gold medallion swung on a chain around his neck. He walked by me slowly, taking the chair with the worn cushion facing the door. I sat across from him with my back to the door.

"Nice car," he mumbled.

"Good on these mountain roads," I replied. "Its low center of gravity and elongated undercarriage hug them nice and tight."

Sinclair cleared his throat. "Ask your questions, Mr. Cole."

I figured the interview would be brief, so I jumped right in. "What can you tell me about Sonja Olson?"

"She's dead."

"Did you know her?"

"Yes."

"Were you a friend of hers?"

"No."

"How did you know her?"

He let out a heavy sigh and made a face that told me he'd been through this, many times, maybe a long time ago, maybe recently in his head. It was never going to go away.

"She was a student at BSC back in 1977. I was a member of the Cross Point Players, a community theater group. Sonja would sit by herself in the auditorium and watch us rehearse for 'Hair.' Our last performance was the night before she died."

"Did you ever speak with her?"

"No."

"Did anyone in your theater company ever speak to her?"

"Not that I'm aware of. We heard her playing the piano sometimes, but she always hurried off whenever we arrived and took the stage."

"Did you ever see her with anyone, inside or outside the hall?"

"I never saw her outside the auditorium."

"You claim to be clairvoyant. Is that correct?"

"It's how I make my living."

"I'll take that as a 'yes.' How does it work?"

"I honestly don't know."

"But you just said you're a psychic. You see things."

"Yes. I have the sight. It's a family trait. Some families have overactive sebaceous glands. In other families, the women can grow beards. My family's curse is the sight."

"Meaning insight, like a sixth sense. You can see things others can't. Yet you don't know how it works and you call it a curse. Others would say it's a gift."

"Only those who don't understand its power. It's a mixed blessing. Look around you. What do you see?"

That was easy for me to answer. I could tell the moment I spotted the little log cabin on the hillside, his existence barely cleared the poverty line. Being inside made that even more evident.

"I see a man who has not profited greatly from his gift, if that's what you mean. I see a man who lives a very solitary life."

"I don't choose to live alone, Mr. Cole. I'm forced to. Do you know what it's like to dine in a restaurant and see the fates of those dining around you but be unable to warn them? It's maddening, chaotic, and it'll drive you insane if you let it. Now imagine living with loved ones and having those same thoughts."

"Did you share your vision of what happened to Sonja Olson with the press?"

"I tried to tell the police. They didn't want to hear it."

"And the family?"

"They were secluded, isolated in their grief."

"So ... word just leaked out."

"To no avail, it would seem."

"Do you still stand by what you say you saw?"

"I can't *un-see* what I saw."

"But you didn't see a face? You don't know who the killer was?"

"The sight only allows me to see so much. The view is not usually of my choosing. I don't control it. I can only tell you what I saw."

"Who chooses, then?"

"My view of that event could have come from only one person's perspective. I was seeing it through the eyes of the killer. That's why I could not see *his* face."

"How is that possible?"

"Somehow I connected with a part of him after the murder. Something at the crime scene that he touched, I touched, and his energy flowed into me."

"When you were at the crime scene? What did you touch? Can you remember?"

79

"Not clearly. Especially not now. It's been over forty years."

"Was it the bloody sheet music? Sonja's discarded clothes? The cord that bound her wrists? The muslin piano cover?"

"I would have to say no. Those things, along with the corpse, were all removed by the time I got to the crime scene. Besides, some of those items would have contained her energy, which I definitely wasn't feeling."

"When did you go back to Randall Hall, and why?"

"I went back about a week later to pick up a hat I had left behind when we did the play."

"How about the piano? It's still there now. Did you touch the piano keys?"

"I remember standing by that rickety old thing, wondering how anybody could play it, and thinking it might fall apart if I touched it."

"I know what you mean. I thought the same thing when I saw it yesterday," I said, recalling how I had to brace the one leg with my knee after it shook beneath Rachel's touch. "And are you sure it was a uniform the killer was wearing?"

"Quite sure."

"Some people have theorized you're the killer and your timely psychic insights were intended as sleight of hand to divert attention."

"Because I'm pointing at the police, you mean. Look, I never said it was a cop's uniform. Others have assumed that."

"Could it have been?"

"Of course. It could have been campus security or CPPD, as much as it could have been a military uniform or maintenance uniform. In my mind's eye, the coloring was similar, pants and shirt alike. And male. I think we can safely exclude a female aggressor because of the force of the trauma to the victim."

"So, it comes down to who had access to her? The possibilities seem both limited and limitless."

"Precisely, which leaves you and the police with very little to go on. Motivation is elusive, yet it is the key to solving this puzzle. One has to assume the means to facilitate the act was disposed of cleanly at the time."

"No weapon has ever turned up anywhere, even during the recent dredging of Lake Erasmus."

Johnson clapped his hands together. "There you have it. Some psychic I am. I'm afraid I haven't been much help to you, Mr. Cole. You came here looking for answers and are leaving emptyhanded."

Message received. The interview was over. No more questions.

"Thanks for your time, Mr. Johnson. I'm sure this hasn't been easy for you."

I got up to leave and stretched out my hand. We shook hands, a formality we neglected when I first arrived. As we shook, Johnson Sinclair held my grip a little longer than I thought natural. Was it my imagination, or did he seem to tense up? Unfortunately, I could not see beyond the red eyeglass lenses to read what his eyes might be saying.

He eventually let go of my hand and walked me to the door, opening it up fully. Then suddenly he stopped and grabbed my forearm tightly.

"He's alive, Mr. Cole. The killer. You need to be extremely careful. He knows you're onto him."

14

I was still shaking as I hurtled down from the mountain hideaway, taking the winding curves blindly and at a speed unsafe for a freight train. Sinclair's parting comments, combined with his intense handshake had me quaking in my walk-softened desert boots. A thousand thoughts swam through my head. *The killer is alive! He knows I'm onto him. Care must be taken ...*

Was the warning some kind of parlor trick? Had Sinclair conjured it up to deflect any further interest I might have in connecting him to this case? Or did he really know something? Did he sense something? If I were to accept his "gift" at face value, where was it coming from? When and where did he—and apparently I—pick up the energy, the vibe, that has me on the killer's track?

And what track is that? Exactly who is the killer? Sinclair didn't come right out and say. Like his faceless, uniformed assailant from decades ago, I've been confronted with a big unknown. But if the killer is alive and I represent a threat to him after all this time, I need to be careful. So why did I not know who it was? And why didn't I ask Sinclair when I had the chance? Maybe I should drive back there and ask him, hound him if I must for the name. If he does know, it's unfortunate and unfair that he's left me feeling vulnerable.

But then, maybe he doesn't know. He said his insights are limited. Yes, he's picking up energy from somewhere, but from where? More important, from whom? If what he's said about his gift is true, that it's all about the flow of unseen energy, then that means we've connected to it, that I've connected to it, and that the killer's connected to it. All three of us.

I tried to think when or where that might have been. If Sinclair didn't know, how was I supposed to figure it out? He's the psychic. I'm just the lowly detective. What's needed here is not psychic energy, but good old-fashioned logic. What's needed is for someone like me to connect the dots.

If I believed in all this paranormal hocus pocus, it would mean the dots represent someone or something we both have come into contact with, that leads straight back to the killer. I could not begin to sort out who or what that might be for Johnson Sinclair. But, who or what could that be for me, assuming it was someone or something linked to the past, forty-four years ago? The pool of possibilities was far fewer. So that's where I concentrated. I'd only been in Cross Point three days. Logic would suggest the contact occurred during that brief time.

The list amounted to no more than five: Rose Lynwood, Rachel Lynwood, Ray Chang, Mark Abrams, and Hugh Bennett. If I eliminated the women, as I felt certain I should, that left Chang, Abrams, and Bennett. Abrams and Bennett would have been kids in 1977, and Chang wasn't even born. So, who was I missing?

The thought occurred to me that I should probably put Johnson Sinclair on the list. He was certainly the right age, and he was there when the crime occurred. But it was his warning to me that was alerting me to the danger. Why would he risk exposing himself now, having gotten away with it for all these years?

No, it simply couldn't be Sinclair. Somewhere in my mind, I'd already dismissed him from the shifting blame brush others painted him with forty-four years ago. In our conversation, he had struck me as forthright and honest. But, if he knew the identity of the killer, why wouldn't he just come out and say so? Unless ... it really was him.

* * * * * * *

It was getting late, and I needed to turn to other matters—namely, letting Rachel know I was headed back to town and setting up a dinner date as promised. I also wanted to brief her on some of the things I'd uncovered, particularly the Sinclair "coincidence" and my chilling interview with him. But first I had to call Mary to get Rachel's number. I called from the car.

"Hey, Mare. Thanks for the info on Johnson Sinclair. I just left his place. The interview went well."

"I'm glad I could help, Mac." She sounded upbeat. That was a good sign.

"How was dinner last night?"

"Free. Drinks included. All I had to do was show up and listen to Audrey complain about Leo. Seems he's growing needy and infantile in his old age."

"That can happen to seniors, especially after they retire. Leo needs a hobby."

"There's not much he's into. Sports, maybe, but Audrey's not."

"Has he tried chasing women?"

"Okay, Mac, stop beating around the bush. What do you really want?"

"You said you gave Rachel Lynwood your cell number to use in emergencies ..."

"Yes ..."

"She didn't happen to give you hers, at the same time? For emergencies, I mean?"

"You can quit the act, Mac. I can hear the panic in your voice. This is the emergency, right?"

"More like a bind."

"Someone has to play gatekeeper when it involves the firm."

"You mean 'stand guard.' I do appreciate it ... most of the time."

"Call it what you want. It's worked so far, hasn't it?"

"Point made, Mary."

"I'm not so sure, Mac. How much longer are you going to stay up there in Podunk, PA?"

"At least through the weekend."

"It's so industrious a place that people work through weekends?"

"No, but I do. The number, please, Mary. I promise to keep a lid on the firm's finances."

"That's not the pot that needs watching."

"I've got a firm grip on what's cooking up here," I lied.

"Just make sure it's *your* hand stirring the pot."

◦ ◦ ◦ ◦ ◦ ◦ ◦

It took some finesse, but Mary finally shared Rachel's cell number with me, as I knew she would. No doubt, I was the reason she acquired it to begin with. Smart girl.

She knew it would be useful one way or another. And she was right.

Mary was a real gem. Her bark was worse than her bite ... because she had no bite. In our years together I'd come to believe she didn't have a mean bone in her body or a negative thought in her head. How she had stayed single was beyond me. Of course, more than one would-be suitor had reported she was married to her job. Their loss was my gain.

Mary was highly protective of me, despite my own lackadaisical attitude at times. She was my right hand, my gal Friday, ever since day one, when we both left our long-held jobs at Axiom Mutual, albeit for different reasons. I was let go as a result of a corporate merger that I later came to find out was actually a hostile takeover by a foreign concern. She left in protest over the hundreds of employees who lost their jobs in the fallout. That was the core of my Mary's heart, although I suspected her feelings for me ran a little deeper and in a slightly different direction than mine did for her.

Rachel Lynwood sounded genuinely pleased to hear from me when I called. She might have been relieved that Mary had given me her number without hesitation, intrigue, or drama. Well, Rachel could go on thinking that. And now she had my number, too.

She was very appreciative of the "cute" note I had sent to her room via Mark, the owner, and grateful to have her iPad back in one piece. I told her it had been useful during my time in the library and I had lots to tell her and her mother about what I'd learned over the past forty-eight hours.

We agreed to meet at the Whistling Pines Tavern around eight o'clock. I was told Saturday night was generally a festive occasion at the watering hole and to be prepared for live music, a Montreal rub rib-eye, refreshing drinks that would make Nick Falcone envious, lively dinner conversation, and a beautiful companion to walk home afterward. My pulse sped up when I realized what might be waiting at the end of that short walk home.

I arrived in Cross Point a few minutes late, thanks to a road closure on the way. The Happy Orchard Inn and the Whistling Pines Tavern were right next to each other. They shared one big parking lot. To save time, I pulled up to the front of the Whistling Pines Tavern and reluctantly turned my Jag over to the young valet. I instructed him to park the car in the corner nearest the Inn and warned him not to leave a single fingerprint on her.

I found Rachel sitting at the bar, talking to a man with his back to me. She excused herself as soon as she spotted me and rushed off to grab the *maître d'*, who signaled for us to follow him. He led us to a quiet booth in the back of the restaurant, far from the noisy atmosphere at the bar. The jacketed host removed the "Reserved" placard and handed us each a menu.

When we were comfortably seated, Rachel set her cocktail down and reached for my hand. "I was beginning to worry about you, Mac. Then I heard some people at the bar talking about a fender bender on Route 601 and figured that might be the hold up. I understand people were hurt. I'm just glad it wasn't you."

"There was a detour. I should have called," I said apologetically. "Unfamiliar roads. I kept thinking I was closer than I was."

The server reappeared. I ordered a Jack on the rocks and another cucumber mojito for Rachel.

"Sorry I didn't have time to change. I hope you'll take pity on me and dispense with soap jokes for an evening."

"You look fresh as a daisy to me. You must be hungry," she said, turning to the menu.

"Famished," I acknowledged.

When the drinks arrived, we raised our glasses in a toast. "I'm down for the whole deal, tonight, sweetheart," I said with a devilish grin. "So, let's get the party started."

"Hear, hear," she replied as we drank.

I set my drink down and looked past Rachel's left shoulder, into the bar. As I did, I noticed the man Rachel had been talking to get up to leave. His back was still to me, but after he paid his bill, he turned and scanned the dining room before he walked out.

"The man you were talking to at the bar is leaving," I said nonchalantly, curious to see her reaction. She continued to study her menu. "Rachel?"

"Hm?"

"Who was that man you were talking to at the bar when I came in? He just left."

"Oh. That was Shelly Hardwick. I thought you met him at the funeral. No, wait a minute. Sorry. That's right. You did tell me you didn't know Ryan had a younger brother."

I stared at Rachel, mystified. I didn't know what the younger Hardwick brother looked like until now.

"Sheldon Hardwick was the shabby, inquisitive guy who followed me around Ryan's funeral service. He introduced himself to me only as 'Shelly.' He never let on he was related to the deceased, and I never put two and two together."

"Trust me, you're not missing much."

"What did you two talk about?"

"He wanted to buy me a drink. I told him I already had one and I was waiting for someone. I've always thought Shelly had a hard-on for my mother. Now I think he's moved on to me."

"That's what you get for running with an older crowd," I joked, although I couldn't help feeling the joke was on me. Not knowing who he was until now gave him a clear advantage over me. No wonder he was so inquisitive at the service.

"Just my luck," chuckled Rachel. "Why couldn't it be Brad Pitt?"

"Wish I'd known who he was before we sat down. I could have made an appointment to ask him a few questions."

"Don't trouble yourself, Mac. If Sheldon Hardwick wanted you to know who he was, he would have made a point to tell you. As for asking him questions, you can generally catch him five days a week at the post office, and seven nights a week in here."

Dinner was as delicious as promised, and the dinner companion lively and engaging. We talked a little shop. I gave her a summary of my time at TPD headquarters yesterday morning, poring over the police transcripts. I even mentioned O'Malley's theory, that the killer could be a member of the CPP cast or crew.

I then went on to pitch the "coincidence" of Johnson Sinclair being both a member of the theatrical troupe and the psychic whose version of the crime now blanketed the internet. She seemed to perk up at the notion that her mother's Ryan Hardwick accusation might be the result of some guilty clairvoyant's sleight of hand, but when I went through my conversation with Sinclair from earlier, she seemed less convinced than I that his story was on the level.

I stopped short of telling Rachel about his parting words to me. That might have made her more empathetic, but maybe not. I found myself swinging back and forth on the idea, so why wouldn't she?

We had a few laughs over my conversation with Nick the bartender, and his take on the "characters of Cross Point," as I referred to them. She felt his assessments of each were pretty much "dead nuts on," with the exception of her father, Carter Lynwood. He remained an enigma to her. She felt he was considerate when it came to her mother but not doting, which Rose would never have stood for, anyway. Her opinion of him was he was unabashedly immersed in academia his whole life, and she let it go at that. That might help to explain his negative feelings about Nick, whom he thought never took his studies seriously.

We lingered longer than many of the other diners, polishing off a second bottle of wine and ending our repast with coffee and a Fra Angelico cordial. I picked up my keys at the valet station but told him to leave the car where it was. We didn't have far to go, and I wanted to savor every step to the Inn.

Outside, Rachel tenderly hooked her arm through mine as we walked. The moon and stars were playing peekaboo with the clouds and the night air was warm and comforting. If we had been paying attention, we would have found the distance was less than fifty yards to where we were going. In that time, our eyes told each other everything we needed to know. The only decision left to be made was her room or mine. Hers won, because it was the closest.

15

All thoughts of ravenous pawing and falling into bed were dashed the moment Rachel switched on the light. Her room was totally trashed.

The fluffy pillows were ripped and gutted, the comforter shredded, the mattress on the floor. Drawers were left open, clothing scattered everywhere. Upset lamps had broken bulbs.

"Oh, my God!" exclaimed Rachel. "What the hell happened here?"

"I'd say it's time for Mark and Hugh to look for a new maid service," I joked, feeling a little tipsy and liking it.

"I'm serious, Mac," said Rachel, running to where the writing desk lay overturned. "My laptop and iPad! They're gone!"

"Don't touch anything," I said firmly, suddenly processing the gravity of the situation. I picked up the phone with my handkerchief and dialed the front desk. Hugh answered.

"We've got a situation in Room 7. Vandalism and theft. Call the police. Then get your ass up here. Pronto."

"This is obscene, Mac," cried Rachel. "Who would do such a thing? For what reason?"

A few things ran through my mind, but I thought it better to wait until the manager arrived. I had a couple of questions for him. "Check and see if anything else is missing, Rachel, but watch where you step."

By the time the authorities arrived, Rachel had determined nothing else was missing. On a hunch, I checked my room, and found everything undisturbed. Whoever went apeshit had constrained his anger and thievery to Room 7.

"I'm so sorry," said Hugh Bennett, his normally jovial face ashen as he surveyed the damage. Mark Abrams gently placed his partner's head on his shoulder. "There, there, Hugh. Everything's going to be fine. We'll get it all cleaned up."

Mark turned his attention to Rachel. "We are very sorry, Ms. Lynwood. Nothing like this has ever happened before. We're going to make it right for you. As soon as you can collect your things, we'll move you to the Presidential Suite downstairs. No extra charge."

Rachel gave me a wistful look. This wasn't the time or place.

A stocky Cross Point officer with short-cropped mousy brown hair crossed the threshold into the room like she owned the place. A younger officer wielding a clipboard followed her.

"What's happened here?" barked the female officer.

"Oh, Jo, we're so glad you're here," gushed Hugh. "Look what someone did to our lovely room!"

"Whose room is it?"

"Mine, Jo," said Rachel.

"I heard you were back in town," said Jo, none too friendly.

"Nice to see you, too," Rachel retorted with similar distain. I didn't need to be a rocket scientist to catch the drift. The bad blood between the two women was thicker than the room's wood-paneled walls.

"Is there anything missing?" the officer questioned.

"My electronic devices."

"Cell phone?"

"No, I had that with me."

Jo put her hands on her hips in a gesture I took to mean she was assuming command of the situation. "Piss off anyone lately, Rachel?"

"In this town? Get in line."

"Who's this?" Jo inquired with a glance my way.

"McKenzie Cole, meet Jo Ellen Hunter, Cross Point's police chief."

She kept her eyes trained on me. "You the guy from Trenton?"

"You the one trying to fill Lionel Hardwick's shoes?" I replied in kind.

Chief Hunter snorted. "I ask the questions. What brings you to Cross Point, Mr. Cole?"

"I have a thing for sycamores in springtime."

"Funny guy. You must be a comedian."

"He's looking into something for Rose," Rachel interjected.

"You don't say."

Chief Hunter looked back at me. "You staying in town?"

"Room 8. Right down the hall."

"You been here all night?"

"We just got in."

"We?"

"Mac and I had dinner together at the Whistling Pines," said Rachel, folding her arms. She came over and stood beside me, daring Jo Ellen to probe further. She obviously did not relish telling Chief Hunter or anyone else in town more than they needed to know about her personal life. "There a law against that?"

"I can vouch for them," Hugh meekly volunteered, trying to diffuse the situation with his affable manner.

"All right, Matthews," said Chief Hunter, addressing her deputy. "You know what to do."

She turned back to Rachel and me. "I'll need you to come down to the station tomorrow, Rachel, for a full statement. Also, I'll need a list of what's missing and the total value." To me, she added, "Don't leave town. I may have more questions for you."

As the two cops set about processing the crime scene, I pulled Rachel out into the hallway. "I'll give you a hand getting your things together," I said in a low, calm voice.

"That's not necessary, Mac. I've had a lovely time. But I think we should call it a night."

"Then I'll go down to the station with you tomorrow."

She gave me a tender kiss on the cheek. "We'll see. Goodnight, Mac."

I waited for Rachel to reenter the desecrated room. Dejected, I turned and shuffled down the hall to my room. My buzz was long gone, and so was my excitement. Our big night together was a bust, but I remained hopeful.

◆ ❀ ❀ ❀ ❀ ❀ ◆ ◆

The knock on my door came at seven-twenty-three in the morning, according to the alarm clock beside my bed. After the poor sleep I had had, the sound brought a smile to my face. It was a little early for my taste, but if Rachel was in the mood for an early morning romp, who was I to complain?

I stood, stretched, and yawned. Sleepy-eyed and becoming aroused, I made my way in wrinkled pajamas to the door. When I opened it, Hugh Bennett blushed a thousand shades of red.

"Sorry to trouble you, Mr. Cole, but I thought you might like to know your Jaguar is about to be towed away."

"It's what?"

"I'm not sure why you decided to leave it in front of the Happy Orchard Inn overnight, but there is a two-hour parking limit on Main Street that's strictly enforced."

"I didn't park it there," I shouted. "Stop them, Hugh. I'll get dressed."

Hugh ran off. I spied my car keys on the nightstand. I threw on a pair of slacks and a polo shirt, slipped on my Clarks, grabbed the keys and ran for the stairs.

I caught up with the flustered owner-manager outside on the street. The Jag was gone.

"We're too late," moaned Hugh.

"Where are they taking it?"

"To the police impoundment lot."

"Where's that?"

"The garage behind the station, on Birch Street."

"Call me a cab."

"No need," yelled Rachel, screeching up to the curb in her Karmann Ghia. "Get in."

"I couldn't sleep," she said, shifting through the gears. "What's going on?"

"Someone is going to great lengths to make things unpleasant for us."

"Why?"

"To discourage us."

She gave me a dumb look. "From what?"

"Doing what we're doing."

"Seeing each other?"

"Poking around a stink hole fearful the foul stench will spread."

"Who knows what you're investigating?"

"Who doesn't? You said it yourself. There are very few secrets in Cross Point. Chief Hunter knew where I was from. It's a good bet she knows why I'm here."

"Are you saying the police are behind this?"

"Given this town's history, I'd say they might be complicit."

"Who's their informant?" Rachel blurted out. "How did they move your car, when you had the keys?"

"Not the entire night. They sat on the valet rack at the Tavern during dinner."

"Oh, my God. Eddie the college kid?"

"Someone could have slipped him a twenty and made a duplicate."

"Okay, but how'd they get into my room? I had the key the whole time."

"Cross Point isn't exactly a hotbed of criminal activity. The Inn is an old building. The room locks are ancient. A penknife like the one I carry around is all you would need."

"So, you think the two incidents are related?"

"I'd be very surprised if they weren't. What was on your computer, Rachel?"

"About the Olson case? Just some notes and a draft outline."

"And the iPad?"

"Whatever you downloaded at the library."

"A handful of old news articles."

"Not much to go on."

"Enough to know what we're up to. I'm sure they know about our visit to Randall Hall, too."

"That still doesn't tell us who's behind it."

"No, but I'm betting we can get your friend Chief Hunter to help us with that. Try to control your feelings for her, will you?"

"Yeah, right!"

16

"Two hundred bucks!" I was livid. "That's outrageous!"

Chief Hunter stood her ground. "That's the fine for parking illegally on Main Street."

"I didn't park there."

She was unmoved. "You're the owner. You're responsible. It doesn't matter how it got there."

"This is police harassment. I won't pay it."

"Perhaps you would prefer to spend the night in one of our cozy Cross Point luxury cells."

"For what offense?"

"Failure to pay your parking fine."

"I won't pay. It's a matter of principle."

"Suit yourself. Matthews, lock him up."

The deputy took a step from behind the counter.

"Stop it, both of you," shouted Rachel. "I'll pay it."

"Don't you dare," I demanded.

"Would you rather spend the night in jail?"

I was flustered. "What's your problem, Hunter? I can understand some level of animosity toward Rachel, the way things are in this town, but what's your beef with me?"

"It's called law enforcement. You break the law, you suffer the consequences."

"Your gang sure got on top of that parking ordinance in a hurry this morning. Just after seven on a Sunday. The roosters don't get up that early in Cross Point."

"We need to keep the streets clear for our churchgoers. If you don't like the way we do things here, you can hightail it back to Trenton."

"You're also well informed, Chief. My hat's off to your information network."

"There's no magic to it, Cole. No wizard behind the curtain. A stranger waltzes into town, attends a brother's funeral, and keeps to himself. We find out this guy is a private investigator from Trenton. At the same time, out of the blue we get a request from the TPD to share our files on an old dead-end case. Cross Point may seem like the sticks to you, but we're not fucking clueless."

"Enough," shouted Rachel, slapping two crisp Franklins on the counter. "Here's the money, Jo. You got my statement and list of missing items. Give Cole the release for his car, and we'll be on our way."

Hunter nodded to Officer Matthews. He stamped the release and handed it to me. "You should listen to your girlfriend more often," he said. "She knows how things work around here."

I wanted to scream. I wanted to let loose an expletive-laced rant but realized that would be pointless. Hunter would never budge. She was a by-the-book law enforcement officer when the book supported her position. But she didn't have to be smug about it. Rachel was right. Spending the night in the Cross Point jail wouldn't accomplish anything.

Rachel drove me around back to the police garage. She could see fumes shooting from my ears. "I know you're frustrated, Mac. You just have to realize you're not going to get any help from the CPPD."

"I wasn't expecting any. This treatment only justifies what you and your mother have contended all along. But I got what I what I wanted to know out of it. The informant was Sheldon Hardwick. Had to be. He saw me at the funeral. I told him where I was from. A simple internet search would do the rest."

"And the room wrecker?"

"Nick characterized Shelly as 'creepy, scary, spooky.' That sound like him to you?"

"That fits. But why attack me and steal my personal belongings?"

"How's jealousy work for you? Maybe because he saw you with me? Is that too much of a stretch?"

"I wouldn't have thought so until you just said it. Who knows what's in his perverted mind?"

"Tell me something, will you? What's the source of the irritation between you and Jo Ellen Hunter?"

"She's a Hardwick. Need I say more? She's Ryan and Shelly's niece through their sister, Sheila."

"That makes Lionel her grandfather. It seems nepotism looms large in the police force at Cross Point. But why would Lionel pass over his eldest son Ryan for the promotion and give the top spot to his granddaughter?"

"I get the impression the old man was disappointed in his sons. When Jo Ellen returned from two tours in Afghanistan, she was different: tough as nails, no nonsense. We used to be friends. You've seen how she is now. I think he liked that attitude in a cop."

"Yeah, like she's one of the guys. She has that military bearing. I'm sure that could have been what Grandpa was looking for. Someone who would crack the whip. But the boys weren't wimps."

"No, but the old man could only cover for them for so long. I think he was afraid of what would happen when he was gone."

My phone pinged just as I was about to jump out of her VW to retrieve my Jag. "It's a text from Mary," I announced, scanning the message. "Johnson Sinclair left a voicemail at the office. Mary monitors it even on weekends. To her, a client is money, any day of the week. Sinclair wants me to call him as soon as possible."

I dialed the number for Sinclair she'd put in the text.

"Hello!"

"This is Cole. I got your message." I threw a wink to Rachel. "I've got you on speakerphone. I'm in the car with my assistant. What's up?"

"Apologies for the short notice. I've been thinking about our conversation the other day. Certain things are beginning to come back to me. If I can run down there today, is there any chance you can get me on the BSC campus?"

Rachel nodded. "Yes," I replied.

"Do you think we can get into Randall Hall?"

Rachel hesitated, then nodded again. "I think so," I said.

"Okay. Did you tell me that stage piano is still where it once was?"

"Yes, and the floor is original, too, just varnished over a couple hundred times. That's what we've been told. The piano certainly looks worn enough to be forty years old."

"All right. Let's say two p.m. today? I'll meet you outside the south entrance."

"Johnson, is there anything else I should know?"

"Probably, but I'm going to save it until I see you. I don't trust cell phones."

He hung up and I shook my head. "That was odd," I admitted to Rachel. "I certainly wasn't expecting to hear from him ever again."

"Do you think we can trust him?"

"At this point, I don't think we can trust anyone."

"Agreed. Say, why don't I meet you back at the Inn? You can leave your car there. In the parking lot this time, please! We'll grab a quick bite at McKenna's and I'll drive us back to BSC."

"Yes, I do believe you'll make a fine assistant one day," I said as I jumped out.

* * * * * * *

We found Johnson Sinclair sitting in his Ford Econoline Van, parked under a shady sycamore tree with the cargo door open, waiting for us.

"What's so urgent?" I inquired as we pulled up.

"Our conversation the other day released a flood of images imploring me to revisit the crime scene," he said, hopping out of the van and sliding the door shut behind him. He was dressed summer-of-love casual with bamboo sandals, worn dungarees and a tie-dye tee shirt. A black silk scarf hung around his neck, entangled in his medallion.

"Johnson, this is Rachel Lynwood. My assistant. Her mother is ..."

"Rose Lynwood," he finished for me. "No need for the subterfuge, Cole. I could have guessed. The physical similarities are striking, but not the temperament, I'll wager?"

Rachel rolled her eyes. "You know my mother?"

"Indeed. From the many years her picture graced the society pages of the *Cross Point Stitch*. As for your temperament, I've followed your career through several of your insightful columns. The one you did last year for the *San Francisco Chronicle* on the extinction of the ivory-billed sand pecker was priceless."

"Well, thank you," she said modestly. "I wish I had known about their plight ten years earlier. We might have been able to save them."

I had to admit, I was mildly impressed with them both, the writer and her admirer. I felt a pang of jealousy thinking I really didn't know much about either of them.

"How do you want to play this, Cole?" asked Sinclair, striding up to our car. "How do we do this without being too conspicuous? The less attention the better, if you know what I mean."

I did. "We'll follow Rachel's lead. She seems to have a way with campus security. Once we get inside Randall Hall, it's your show."

Sinclair toyed with his ponytail and fussed with his beard. Straightening his beret in the VW sideview mirror, he asked, "Shall I drive?"

"No," replied Rachel before I could. "If you don't mind sprawling out in the back seat, we'll go in my car. The campus police are big boys who watch too much 'NCIS.' The van may draw undue scrutiny."

"Sounds like a plan," agreed Sinclair. He locked up his van and jumped in.

We entered the main gate, stopping at the guard station. Brandon, the pimple-faced guard, smiled at the sight of Rachel. She beamed back.

"Is it me, or some other attraction that keeps you coming back to the old campus?" the security guard flirted, no doubt wishing it were the former but knowing it was not.

"Oh, it's definitely you, Brandon," Rachel said, playing along, "and I brought along friends to finish our grand tour. I expect things are still pretty quiet around here on Sundays?"

"Not lately," Brandon confessed. "That construction incident last week has the administration in a tizzy. Construction of the new security building is running behind schedule, so the contractor stepped it up by working weekends, and we've had to ramp up security along with it."

"Chang must be beside himself," teased Rachel.

"He is, because it means he has to be here, too. You can find him at the new Tanner building that's going up on the periphery of Parking Lot A. Beware, he's not in a good mood."

"Is he ever?" I tossed out. Brandon chuckled politely as he handed us visitor tags.

Rachel drove through the gate onto Campus Drive and into Parking Lot A, on the western end of campus. Further west, the girded structure that would become Tanner Hall stood, unfinished. Rachel chose an open parking space in the center of the near-empty lot, about thirty yards from the construction site.

The three of us hopped out of the car. But we didn't get far. Chang spotted us and ran toward us from the construction site.

"Stop right there!" he said, throwing up his hands. "Only authorized personnel with hard hats on are permitted beyond this point."

"That's fine with us, Ray," said Rachel. "We were looking for you. We just came by to finish our tour since it got cut short by the rain the other day."

Chang glanced at Sinclair dubiously. "I see you brought along another guest?"

"Yes. He missed the first part. So would you mind opening Randall Hall again for us?"

"No can do, Rachel. The shit has hit the fan around here because of that construction incident. Besides, it's Sunday. Brandon should know better. The campus is closed. Only dormitories and essential service buildings are open and accessible."

"We'll only be a few minutes," she pleaded.

"The answer is still no."

I could see the optimism in Rachel's eyes dim. I felt a paternal need to speak up as an idea formed in my head. "Well, then, would you mind if we strolled around the campus on our own? It's a beautiful day, and we've come a long way at the invitation of Rose Lynwood just to see this lovely campus. She promised us BSC would be very accommodating. After all, the school and the board have a reputation for diversity, transparency, and hospitality."

I didn't know if the last part was true or not, but I knew based on our previous visit that the name Rose Lynwood carried clout with the BCS board of trustees.

I could hear the wheels grinding inside Chang's shaved dome. He was already on the administration's radar, working overtime because of the construction commotion. Trouble bubbling up to the board from the revered former provost's wife and daughter might add fuel to the fire. That was a flame he couldn't afford to light.

At length, Chang said, "That you can do. But I'm afraid I can't escort you around. I've got to stay close to the work going on at the construction site at all times."

"Understood," said Rachel. "I can play tour guide."

"Can't let you do that, either, Rachel. You need to be accompanied by a member of our security team."

"Even just to picnic around Lake Erasmus?"

"Even there. But if you are insistent, and can wait, I'll send one of my guys to meet you over at Gwendolyn. He can take you around from there."

We didn't have much of a choice. I knew the plan was to get Sinclair inside Randall Hall, and I was curious about what revelations might result. In the back of my mind, I felt certain we could find a way to shake our campus babysitter somehow and slip into Randall Hall. I turned and gave the others a nod. "Done. We'll wait for your man there." I turned to Rachel and Johnson. "Let's go."

Though stunned, they followed me. Once we got out of sight of Chang, I picked up the pace.

"What do you have in mind, Cole?" questioned Sinclair. The more time I spent time with him, the more I believed this so-called psychic was indeed an intuitive person. He seemed to be aware of my thoughts before I put them into action.

We stopped to catch our breath on the steps of Gwendolyn Hall. I surveyed the area. No security guard in sight, and no one else for that matter.

"Rachel," I said, pulling her aside. "Remember our conversation that first day in the auditorium, about how easy it was to get into Randall Hall when it was locked? You said everybody knew how, even you?"

"Of course," said Rachel, growing demonstrably excited as she caught on. "The bathroom windows. Unless they've been upgraded, they're just big louvers that don't lock."

"Show us."

17

Rachel led us around to the back of Randall Hall. She pointed. "Ladies' room to the right, men's room to the left."

I noticed right away either side would do. The windows hadn't been upgraded.

"These are actually jalousie windows," I explained to her. With no screens and turning cranks, things were shaping up even better for us. Upward pressure on the window from the outside would turn the inside crank in the opposite direction, opening up the window with ease. Fully opened, the horizontal slats were wide enough for a slender person to slip through. I chose the ladies' room.

"You've done this before," I said to Rachel, more as a presumption than a question.

"Once or twice."

"Good enough. Once you get inside, don't turn on any lights. Use the light from your cell phone to guide you to the back door and unlock it. We'll be waiting."

"Got it."

"And hurry. We don't have a lot of time. Security will be here any minute."

Sinclair pulled up on the middle slat of the bathroom window. Gradually, all of the corresponding slats in the window frame fanned open. I gave Rachel a boost. She slipped through the window and tumbled onto the floor. I saw her phone light go on inside and motioned for Sinclair to follow me back to the rear door.

Rachel was a beat ahead of us. Inside I could hear her hands scrabbling at the wooden door. She turned back the bolt and twisted the doorknob. The door creaked opened slowly. We were in.

Closing the door behind us, I borrowed Rachel's phone and advised the other two to follow me single-file into the auditorium. We could not risk turning on any lights that might be seen from the outside. The recessed overhead stage lights should do just fine, I thought.

From the side of the auditorium, we made our way down the center aisle to the stage like a line of pinballs rolling toward a score. Rachel and I hopped up from the catwalk while Johnson did the smart thing and took the side stage steps. I sneaked behind the drawn curtain and flicked on the stage lights.

We watched as Sinclair stood on stage, mesmerized, looking out into the vacant seats. No doubt he was reliving the glorious moments he had on that stage forty-four years ago.

"Back there," he said, pointing to the last seat in a far corner row. "That's where she'd sit, hunkered down, watching us rehearse. The director didn't care. He seemed amused by her and let her stay."

Sinclair lingered a few minutes longer in a trance-like state. We watched as he stood with his eyes closed, arms spread at his sides, his fingers opening and closing in a heartbeat rhythm. A low moan emanated from his lips. Some type of prayer, summoning the spirit of Sonja

Olson, I imagined, to come to us and provide assistance in unraveling the mystery of her death.

Rachel shot me a glance. I could read her expression: *Is he for real?*

"Johnson," I called. When he turned, I pointed to my watch. He nodded.

The three of us walked over to the upright piano stationed at stage right. "Is this it?" asked Sinclair.

I nodded. "And over there in the corner, under the piano cover is where they found the body."

"Wish I had the photographs from the crime scene in front of me," he said tentatively. "Something seems amiss."

"I saw the police photos," I said. "Let me be your eyes. What do you want to know?"

"The blood. Where was the blood?"

"On the white muslin sack in the corner," I said, "soaking through from the body underneath it."

Sinclair turned toward the corner and closed his eyes. "Nothing," he said. "I'm getting nothing."

He turned back to the piano. "How about around the piano?"

"Blood spattered on the sheet music," I said. "Tiny droplets."

"What was the music?" Sinclair insisted. "What was she playing?"

"'Age of Aquarius/Let the Sunshine In.'" I remembered from a closeup of one of the police photos. The upper left-hand corner of the sheet music was torn off but the title of the piece was plainly visible.

"From our play," said Sinclair, sucking in the air. He shook his head. "I don't hear it," he said sadly. "I don't hear music coming from her."

Rachel and I looked at each other, unsure what to think. Was this all a scam, a good piece of playacting, or was that real concern in his voice?

"Time," I whispered to him. The last thing we needed was to be caught trespassing. I had little doubt the campus cop assigned to lead us on the tour had already come and gone at Gwendolyn and reported us missing to Chang.

Sinclair would not be rushed. "What else?" he insisted.

I thought hard. "On the keys," I answered. "There was blood on the piano keys."

Sinclair ran his fingers over the keys. "So many hands," he mumbled with eyes closed. "Hundreds of hands ... and," his eyes opened wide, "yours!" He shouted to Rachel. "Yes, you've played it recently."

Rachel gasped and put her hands to her mouth. I could almost hear her say, *How did he know?*

I was about to say "Time's up," but my lips chose not to utter the words. Instead, I heard Sinclair ask for more. "More, Cole, for heaven's sake. Give me something to work with, here."

I closed my eyes, trying to picture the photos I had examined at TPD headquarters. So many of them contained Sonja's beaten, bloodied face that I didn't want to force my mind to remember.

"The leg," I blurted. "Blood, streaming down the piano leg."

Sinclair concentrated on the piano. "Which leg?"

I stared at the piano. The upright had two pole-like wooden fore legs. There were no back legs. The rear of the piano was a box on tiny wheels. I searched my memory. "The left," I said. "I think it was the one on the left."

"Wait!" shouted Sinclair. "That's it. I see it now. I know what's wrong. This piano is out of position. Quick Cole, give me a hand. We need to move it back about two feet."

I came around the other side of the piano and pushed. Sinclair pushed and guided from the front. The wheels spun easily over the heavily waxed stage floor, but the left leg wobbled and shimmied. When we had the piano in place, Sinclair held up his right had to stop. I tugged backward on the piano like a brake. When I did, the left leg fell to the floor with a *thump* that echoed around the stage. The piano pitched down to the left.

Sinclair and I reached for the leg simultaneously to silence it. His face froze, his hand gripped around the leg. I looked into his eyes. They were glazed over. He was somewhere else. "Let go," he whispered. "Let go of it."

I did what he asked. He shivered, then dropped the leg. It rattled around the room again. When it stopped, he studied it. I followed his gaze, trying to visualize what he was seeing.

The wooden leg was scratched in several places but otherwise not worn down like the rest of the piano. There was a threaded bolt at the top of the leg that screwed up into the underside of the upright piano. The joint must have gotten stripped over time and worked loose, allowing the leg to wobble, like it had when I steadied it with my knee.

"Cole," Sinclair implored quietly. "Carefully put the leg back in place. Don't twist it. Don't turn it. Just slide it up back into place. And take care to handle it from the bottom. Try not to touch it anywhere else. I'll lift it to make it easier for you."

Sinclair's words hit me. It suddenly dawned on me, why his insistence on extra caution. The insight became clearer when I caught a glimpse of the darkened tip of the bolt embedded in the wooden leg.

With the leg back in place, the two of us stood and sighed in unison.

Rachel stood with her arms crossed, looking at us, perplexed. "What's going on?"

"I'll tell you later," I said. At any moment I was expecting Chang to come bursting through the door with half a dozen CPPD cops. "We gotta go. Now!"

I switched off the stage lights and held up my lit phone. We dashed from the stage to the hallway and out the back door. The lock was designed to click in place upon contact with the plate when shut. I ran around to the far side of the hall and re-closed the bathroom windows. No sense leaving a trail. The way my head was spinning, I could already envision a time when we might need this clandestine route of entry again. I hoped not.

As we turned the corner, Gwendolyn Hall came fully into view. Brandon was on the front steps. He waved to us when he saw us coming. We waved back.

"Hey! Where have you guys been? I've been waiting here about twenty minutes."

"Mr. Cole has a prostate problem, Brandon," Rachel offered—which, of course, she probably surmised from my bathroom urgency the morning we met. She waited for me to challenge it. I did not. I was too excited and slightly winded.

"When you've got to go, you've got to go," I added for emphasis, adding an exaggerated look of relief.

"Don't get old," said the sage Sinclair.

"Okay, good advice," acknowledged Brandon hesitantly, although I'm fairly sure he didn't fully comprehend the alternative to growing old Sinclair's comment alluded to. "Are you guys ready to resume your tour?"

"I think we're going to have to take a rain check, Brandon, all things considered," said Rachel.

"Yes, we'll come back when the campus is a bit more lively and accessible," I said, adding a specific reason for our sudden turnabout. "It's dead around here on Sundays."

"And we'll request you specifically for the tour," Sinclair added for flavor.

Rachel placed a hand tenderly against Brandon's inflamed cheek and smiled deeply. It was a gesture of gratitude for a boy who no doubt lacked female attention. We said our "so long" and hurried off.

18

Exhausted, the three of us ended up at the Whistling Pines Tavern a half-hour later, in the same booth Rachel and I had shared the night before. I couldn't help thinking what a difference a day made, and yet that really didn't begin to cover what had happened in the last twenty-four hours.

I could see Rachel was desperate for information. I didn't know if she was truly clueless or whether she, like us, was looking for affirmation of what we all just experienced.

She ordered a cucumber mojito and had it half drained before a word was spoken. I was game to keep pace with my Jack on the rocks, but Sinclair exercised a little more self-control, nursing a frosty Michelob Ultra. For Rachel's benefit, Sinclair and I were purposely silent on the ride back to town. The car was not the place. Plus, I didn't know about Sinclair, but I knew I still needed to sort things out in my own head.

Like being glued to a tennis match, she glanced from Sinclair to me expectantly. "Well, will somebody please tell me what the hell just happened? And remember I'm a journalist. I'll know if you're jerking my chain."

Sinclair looked at me for guidance. I could see he was struggling with where to begin. So was I. Rachel wasn't having it. She wanted answers. Now.

She glared at Sinclair. "How did you know I played that piano? Did Cole tell you? He told you, right?"

Again, Sinclair looked to me. He cleared his throat.

"I don't fully understand it, myself, but I'll tell you what I told Cole when he asked me how the gift works. The short answer is I don't know. What I do know is it has something to do with energy. Energy is everywhere. Energy is matter and matter is energy. It's all around us.

"Energy in motion, like a fulcrum at work, or a set of car gears, is considered mechanical energy. We see the result of the energy transference in the resulting action. Energy that is stored is like data on a DVD. It's intelligent, even spiritual, but unseen."

Rachel gave me a sharp look to see if maybe Sinclair was pulling her leg. Truth was it seemed logical to me, but maybe not in so many words.

Sinclair continued. "Our bodies are energy vessels that create, store, and emit energy. Every thought, word, and action is a form of that energy. When you played the piano, your mechanical energy produced the music you heard while your spiritual energy got stored in the keys. Both forms were transferred into and out of the piano.

"I am a sensitive. All that means is I can see and feel energy fields around me. Auras, if you like. When I touched certain piano keys, I received a flow of energy from literally hundreds of fingers that had touched those keys, including yours. I got such a rush of it, I knew you had played that piano very recently."

"You could tell all that, just from the few notes I played?"

Sinclair nodded his head. "Afraid so."

"What about that thing with the piano leg? What was going on between you two?"

I waited for Sinclair to answer. I didn't want to spoil any part of the experience—or short-circuit the education we were receiving.

"The leg had energy within it, too," Sinclair confirmed.

Rachel leaned forward. "From Sonja, from her blood?"

"Yes," replied Sinclair. He shot a glance my way. "And more."

"More?" Rachel was on the edge of her seat. So was I, but I tried not to show it. I still had a lot of questions rolling around in my head, like a load of clothes tumbling in a dryer, waiting to come out clean and wrinkle-free.

"I felt Cole's energy."

"Remember how it wobbled when you toyed with it," I said to Rachel. "I put my knee against it to steady it."

Sinclair nodded.

She turned back to me and asked one of the most important questions of the day, hanging in the air. "So, did *you* feel anything when you grabbed the piano leg?"

I lowered my head. "No. I didn't feel anybody's energy. That doesn't mean what Sinclair is saying isn't true. I guess it just means I'm not sensitive."

Rachel chuckled. "I don't need a piano leg to tell me that. I knew that two minutes after I met you." Rachel finished her drink and ordered another round.

She turned her attention back to Sinclair and put her journalism cap back on. "So is that *the* piano?" she asked. "The one in your vision, where you see Sonja Olson being murdered by a man in a uniform?"

He nodded vaguely.

"But you can't or won't identify him?"

Sinclair didn't flinch or protest. In fact, I thought he handled Rachel's verbal attack fairly well.

"As I told Cole, I never claimed to have experienced the murder from Sonja's point of view. In my glimpse into the past, I saw the action through the killer's eyes. I must have touched something he handled during the assault that had his energy stored in it. And now I am certain. I know what that something was. It was the piano leg, and you knew it, too, didn't you, Cole? I could read it on your face."

"Is that why you asked me to put it down?" I said. "You wanted to be sure. You didn't want my energy interfering with the reception you were getting."

"Yes."

"I get it!" exclaimed Rachel. "Holy shit. It wasn't a baseball bat after all. He beat her unconscious with the piano leg. That was the murder weapon. Then he put it back in place."

"Yes," I concurred. I had come to the same conclusion when I reattached the leg. "It's been hidden in plain sight for forty-four years."

"So now we go to the authorities, right?"

"Not so fast, Rachel," said Sinclair. "That's only one small piece of the puzzle. We still need a motive and, more important, a suspect."

"He's right," I agreed. "We are the only three who think we know *how* she was killed. If we go to the authorities prematurely, it might tip off the killer. Besides, the leg is just a theory at this point. Until we can tie that piano leg to either the killer or the victim, it's not evidence. It's just one possible explanation, our version, if you will."

Rachel saw the dilemma. We all did. "So, what do we do?"

Sinclair had been peeling the label off his beer bottle. He was waiting for me to speak up.

"You still think the killer's alive?" I asked him.

"Uh huh."

I probed hard. "How do you know that, Johnson?

"Because you've come in contact with him."

"Wait! What?" said Rachel, squirming in her seat. "Mac, you've met the killer?"

"Indirectly," I conceded, looking for Sinclair to expand.

"The two of you have definitely crossed paths, maybe more than once. The leg confirms it. I could feel the energy from both of you through the piano leg today. That's why I asked you to put it down. Your energy was more recent, stronger. But his was still present from forty-four years ago. It had dissipated but I got the same sensation. I saw the same version of events I told the authorities all those years ago. That's why I called you. I was receiving haunting flashbacks. Something in the hall, on the stage, near the piano I handled back then. But given the media frenzy and the passage of time, it became a blur. It could have been several things. But the link to the killer was definitely the piano leg. We confirmed that today."

"That doesn't necessarily mean he's alive," I said. "If the leg is our connection, I touched it on Thursday when we visited the campus, but the killer we now know handled it forty-four years ago, when you also first handled it."

"That's why I think the contact has been more than once, and recent. When we shook hands at my place yesterday his energy flowed from you, stronger than I felt today from the leg. And more importantly, the intelligence carried in that energy transference told me he was in a state of alarm. Emotions are strong energy sources. He saw you as a threat, even if you don't know who he is yet."

"Could you see him?" I asked, perplexed.

"Not clearly. There seemed to be a lot of people milling around, expanding my view, but also clouding the clarity of the insight."

"So how do we find out who it is? I tried making a list of potential Cross Point contacts. After putting them through all the filters, the closest name I came to was yours."

"That's a good start, but you could have overlooked someone in a crowd."

"Not if the interaction was as strong as you imply. Christ, it's like we'd been intimate or something. Believe me, if it was a man, I would remember."

Rachel had been silent for a long time, listening and thinking hard. Finally, she spoke up.

She directed her question to Sinclair. "We've been so focused on all this talk about energy, aren't we forgetting the science? We all agree we need physical evidence. Energy and psychic visions don't qualify as hard evidence in a court of law. But if the leg *is* the murder weapon, isn't it possible there's some evidence still on it?"

Sinclair nodded. "Perhaps. Though, collecting it and sorting through it could be tricky."

I jumped in. "Collecting it will be a huge problem as long as we keep it to ourselves, as I think we must. But today's technology, with biometric identification systems through fingerprinting and DNA analysis, is lightyears from where it was four decades ago. Hell, DNA didn't even come into common use until the 1980s."

"It's something to think about," agreed Sinclair. "All we need are solid samples and a broad database."

I summarized the situation. "Without the school's consent or CPPD involvement, and without removing the piano leg and sending it off to the lab, it will be extremely difficult.

"In the meantime, Johnson, if we can retain your services for a little while longer after dinner, how would you like to run your energy detector through Rachel's room for us? It was burglarized last night. The police seem incompetent, but we think there might be a connection. Maybe you can help shake things up a bit."

"Hey, I'm game."

19

Following his psychic survey of Room 7, Sinclair came up empty. In the process, however, he did conjure in his extra sensory receptors the essence of Rachel Lynwood, and that of various former Happy Orchard Inn guests, including septuagenarians Alfred and Grace Martindale, who recently celebrated their fiftieth wedding anniversary there, as they had their wedding night. But nothing tangible related to the break-in led to any clear mental pictures.

Whoever trashed her room wore gloves. The police concluded they must have used the back stairs and unlocked the rear door from the parking lot. They also confirmed no prints were found, other than Rachel's, the two owners', and the housekeeper's. Neither Sinclair nor the police had an inkling as to whether it was the work of a single person, or several.

We thanked Sinclair for spending the day and sharing his insights with us. We walked him down to the lobby, where he bade us a fond goodnight. We indicated we would all stay in touch, should anything further develop.

After Sinclair left, Rachel and I found two high-backed Queen Anne chairs in the quiet, empty lobby. We sat by the gas fireplace, taking in the warm, peaceful atmosphere of the wood-paneled room. Hugh Bennett was on call behind the desk. The genial owner put a kettle on for us, and soon we were enjoying a cup of HOI's signature drink, apple cinnamon tea with a dash of Myers rum.

"Do you always do that when you're deep in thought?" asked Rachel, setting her cup and saucer down on her lap. Apparently, she'd been staring at me.

"Do what?" I asked innocently.

"Stroke your mustache," she said, imitating my downward motion with her thumb and forefinger.

"So, I've been told," I replied with a sheepish grin.

"By Mary?"

"Among others. It's an old habit. I guess it's why I was never a good card player."

"What were you just thinking about? Can you share it?"

I set my teacup down. "I was thinking, if Sinclair is right, we can cross Ryan Hardwick off our list of potential killers. The closest I ever came to him was being in the same room as his reliquary urn."

"That's if Sinclair is on the level."

"I can't speak to the accuracy of his gift, but if Sinclair was the killer, I don't see what he stood to gain by going back to the scene of the crime the way he did today. It's not like he was going to dispose of any evidence he left behind forty-four years ago. Not with us there."

Rachel sipped her tea. "Point made."

"In fact, we may have come a step closer to solving this damn thing. I am convinced the piano leg is the murder weapon. When I held it in my hand, it felt like it could do the job rather easily, and I think I spotted dried blood on the embedded bolt at the top."

"Enough for forensics?"

I shrugged. "Worth a try."

"Okay, but how?"

"I've got to get back into Randall Hall. But first I need to make a call to my TPD contacts. Maybe they can confirm how long dried blood cells hold their DNA signature and how much residue is needed for a match. They might also be able to suggest a way to collect and test both fingerprints and DNA without sending the artifact to the lab. I remember hearing something about a mobile fingerprint scanning technique. That would be great if they had something like that for DNA testing, too.

"You said 'I've got to go back into Randall Hall.' What happened to 'we'?"

"I can't run the risk of you getting caught, Rachel. Your family's reputation would suffer greatly."

"Do I seem like the kind of girl who worries about her reputation?"

I laughed, because she was right. "No, but I care."

She stood and yawned, accentuating her lithe limbs and well-proportioned body through her snug tee shirt and tight jeans.

"Old insensitive, you," she said, coming over and planting a tender kiss on my forehead.

She glanced up at the desk to see what Hugh was up to. He had appeared to be reading a salacious novel earlier, but appearances can be deceiving.

"You can just go on thinking and playing with your moustache, Mr. Cole," she added, raising her voice and slowly walking away. "As for me, it's been a long day. Time for this gal to get her beauty rest."

* * * * * * * *

Dave Hart

It was just after midnight when I heard footsteps in the hallway. Soft at first, they grew louder until they stopped at my door. I heard the doorknob turn slowly, followed by the creaking of my door being opened.

A stray sliver of light came in from the hallway. Turning my head halfway, I could see the outline of a shadowy figure creeping ever so cautiously toward me. Another brief pause, then a soft *thump*. With a shiver I could feel the bed covers being gently pulled aside. I turned fully to face the intruder as she slid, naked and warm, into bed beside me.

20

"You took a hell of a chance," said Rachel with a wry smile, "not locking your door last night."

We were sitting in McKenna's Café, having breakfast. Sometime around first light, before our friendly innkeepers rose, Rachel had slipped back into her robe and quietly downstairs to the Presidential Suite, next to their room, unnoticed. After all, she said, a single girl had to keep up the pretense of propriety in a small town like Cross Point, even if it was just an act.

I returned her satisfied smile with one of my own. "There was no risk involved," I said. "I did what a good PI does for a living. I looked for clues."

"So, what gave me away? Was it the kiss on the forehead? Or have you suddenly absorbed some of Sinclair's psychic powers?"

"I'll never tell."

She threw a sugar packet across the booth at me. I ducked.

"Are you going to tell Mother about your suspicions regarding the piano leg?"

"Not just yet. She'll be crushed, so I don't want to burst her bubble until we have a solid alternate suspect."

Rachel stirred her latte. "She knows you're in town. She's gonna want an update."

"I was hoping you might do that for me."

"What are you going to do while I'm stonewalling dear old Rose?"

Before I could answer, I watched as Shelly Hardwick, dressed for work, came striding through the café door. Rachel's back was to him, but I had him in my direct line of sight.

He walked up to the counter and grabbed a coffee in a to-go cup. He paid with cash, then he disappeared back out the door. The whole incident took maybe thirty seconds. He never once looked our way.

"You're doing it again, Mac," said Rachel, snapping her fingers. "What's going on inside that mind of yours?" She turned and glanced toward the door, but Shelly was already out of sight.

I was stroking my mustache again. I tried placing my hand on the table, then I brought both hands up to my face and gave it a good squeeze. Then, like a light bulb suddenly switched on, it clicked. I could have kicked myself for not seeing it sooner. Seeing Sheldon Hardwick on his way to work was the trigger. It was in front of my face the whole time.

"Mac!" shouted Rachel. "Earth to McKenzie Cole, come in please."

I looked at Rachel, wild-eyed. Amazed at my own insight. Maybe I looked as bewildered as she, but for a different reason.

"How well do you know Shelly Hardwick?" I asked, unable to mask the growing excitement in my voice.

"I don't know how to answer that," she replied, caught off guard. "Does this have anything to do with last night?

Because if it does, I can assure you there is nothing going on between Shelly Hardwick and me."

"No, that's not what I mean. Do you have any idea where Shelly might have been forty-four years ago, when trouble came to Cross Point?"

Rachel looked at me like I had two heads. "You're kidding, right? Shelly Hardwick. You want to put Shelly Hardwick on that short list of yours?"

"Why not? He must have been around back then. How old could he have been? Twenty-two, twenty-three?"

"I think I remember Mother saying he was a year or two younger than Ryan."

"There you go. How long has he worked for the post office?"

"Gosh, I don't know, Mac. As long as I've known him, why?"

"Find out. Ask your mother, Rachel. It's important."

"Where is this coming from, Mac? Another epiphany, like last night's clandestine romp?"

"Last night had nothing to do with ESP or inner visions. It was the result of pure unadulterated desire. I wanted you, too. Badly."

"Well, that's a relief."

She finished her latte. "So why do you want to know how long Shelly worked at the post office? Where's this all heading?"

"Think about it, Rachel. The funeral. You weren't there, but I was. The only person I met there was Shelly Hardwick. I talked to him, shook his hand, and that was before I knew who he was."

"Yeah, so?"

"Remember what Sinclair said after he shook my hand. He sensed the killer. Somehow I had interacted with the killer here in Cross Point. Sinclair felt his energy again through me. The same energy he sensed from the piano leg decades ago that precipitated his vision of the crime, and then he felt it again yesterday. Is that really so hard to believe after all these years?"

"That Shelly Hardwick murdered Sonja Olson? Yes!"

"Sinclair also said while reading the energy in your room that he sensed the presence of someone else, maybe someone having the same energy. But the vision was unclear because of the *crowd* around him.

Rachel shot up in her seat. "The funeral service."

"Yes."

"But what about the uniform? Shelly was never in law enforcement or the military, that I'm aware. By 1977 the Vietnam conflict was over, thankfully."

"I agree. But maybe Sinclair couldn't identify the type of uniform because it was so mundane, ordinary. Have you ever seen a postal worker's uniform? It's like a maintenance uniform, only blue."

Rachel caught on instantly. The excitement flowed like a swift-moving stream. "Oh my God! It fits. But how do we prove it? We can't have him arrested on psychic vibrations, and he'll never confess. He'd be a fool to. We have no evidence. We'd never get a conviction, not for a cold case like this, on such slender accusations."

"There may be a way," I said hesitantly. "But I'll need your help."

"Uh oh. How?"

"Find out how long he's worked for the post office, and get his fingerprints."

"Are you nuts? How the hell am I supposed to do that?"

"Have a drink with him. Tonight!"

21

It would not be easy to convince Rachel to meet up with Shelly Hardwick at the Whistling Pines Tavern for a casual drink. Her distain for him was palpable. I certainly hadn't sweetened the prospect with my accusation that he was a killer.

So I suggested she talk with her mother first, find out what she could from Rose about Shelly, especially regarding his tenure with the Postal Service and his whereabouts during the period in question. If nothing fit, she was off the hook.

But if the information jived with our hypothesis, then she should go ahead and set up the encounter. It need not be complicated. As she had pointed out, Shelly could be found at the bar nightly. She could just, sort of, naturally bump into him like she had on Saturday night. If she could do that much, I'd take care of the rest.

She tentatively agreed to the plan, and we parted—she to see her mother, and I to make the first of two important phone calls.

"Christ, Mac, you still hanging around Podunk County?" Bill Perkins was never one to mince words. Not with me.

"Still here, Bill."

"You on vacation or something? We figured you'd have it solved by now, especially after O'Malley ran it down for you while you were here."

"As only O'Malley can," I said, exasperated by the mere thought.

"So, what can we do for you now?" The chief sounded ebullient. That was good, given what I was about to ask of him.

"I need a crash course in the latest police forensic techniques."

"Forensics?" Perkins hooted. "Don't tell me you dug up the corpse."

"Not the body, Bill, but maybe some of the blood."

"Where's it been hiding for four decades?"

"Concealed on a piano leg. Crusted on a bolt joint and hidden in place. I'm thinking the piano leg might be the long-lost murder weapon."

I could just imagine Perkins laughing to himself on the other end. "Now *that* sounds promising. What do you want to know?"

"How long is blood DNA good for?"

"Has it been kept in a dry place?"

"Room temperature, no moisture, no light."

"Sounds right. How much material have you got?"

"Not much. A few scrapings at best."

"Well, I'm no expert, but if you want to bring the article in here, we'll see what we can find on it. Reminds me of this recent case in France. Serial rapist-killer who went on a rampage in the early nineties and was never caught.

The Paris police kept some of the material evidence from the crime scenes in custody, hoping for an eventual breakthrough. And there was. As technology advanced, they narrowed the field of suspects. Eventually DNA taken from the sanitary napkin of one of the victims pointed to one of their own, a retired Paris cop. As the net began to close around him, he committed suicide. A postmortem DNA test confirmed he was the serial killer."

"That's a nice bedtime story, Bill, but I'm afraid I can't bring you the actual item."

"Oh, no. Planning to pass over the locals and go straight to the FBI?"

"Negative. It would be your baby exclusively, if you want it. It's just that I can't bring you the item with the DNA material attached to it. I'll have to collect it in the field."

"I see. Chain of custody could be an issue. But, suppose the material is sufficient, and you manage to keep it undiluted while collecting it? I assume we're trying to get a match with the victim. Where is the comparison DNA coming from, if not from the corpse?"

"Good question, Bill. I hadn't really thought about that."

"Does the victim have any living relatives?"

"A younger sister somewhere."

"That'll at least get us in the genetic ballpark. What else have you got? Any prints?"

"Not unless you tell me there's some kind of magic mobile fingerprint scanner that you guys use?"

"There is. Works like the camera on a smart phone."

"Can the device read in the dark?"

"It comes equipped with an ultraviolet light. Or you can dust the article with radioactive isotopes, if you prefer." He chuckled loudly. He had a maniacally dry sense of humor and knew all the right buttons to push.

"You don't happen to have a mobile fingerprint scanner with UV capability ... *in-house*, do you?"

"No. We have two."

"That's swell, Bill. What are the chances of my secretary picking one up from the station this afternoon? I promise to return it tomorrow."

"Zero, Mac. The device comes with a ninety-eight-hundred-dollar price tag. The mayor would have my badge if it got lost or broken by a layperson on an out-of-district case."

"I appreciate the dilemma."

"Tell you what. O'Malley's already got his feet wet with this case. I'm prepared to send him up with it. I'm sure he'd enjoy the pleasant countryside drive. Do him good, and you get both the scanner and O'Malley's expertise."

"You make it sound so appealing. How can I refuse?"

"Listen to me, Mac. I don't know what your deal is with the CPPD. I sincerely hope you can work things out. Meanwhile, I'd sure like to keep TPD's nose clean on this whole affair. O'Malley's not a guarantee, but at least we'll have a hand in the game."

I didn't like the idea at all, but I could see no other choice. "That's more than fair, Bill. I promise we'll try not to kill each other."

While I was less than excited about bringing Detective O'Malley more fully on board (hadn't I suffered enough with him?), Bill Perkins had once again proven to be a good friend and a cagey police chief, which was more than I could say about the CPPD Chief Jo Hunter. As far as I could tell, she wanted my head on a silver platter and didn't care who delivered it.

If I thought the call to Chief Perkins was a strategic victory, the next call to Mary Porter would ask of her an act of faith beyond anything I'd asked before. I caught her just as she was about to leave the office for lunch.

"Hello, Mary."

"Hello, Mac. How are things? Any progress?"

"Actually, yes, a big breakthrough. That's why I'm calling."

"Let me guess, you need me to do something big?" I could hear the excitement in Mary's voice. She loved getting her hands dirty when a little intrigue was involved.

"Actually, two things."

"I'm listening."

"First, I need you to use your Google skills and see if you can locate a woman named Karin Olson who lived in Alameda, California, back in the late seventies. She'd have been in her early twenties around 1977 and is probably in her late sixties now if she's still alive. Both parents were educators, her father a professor at Swarthmore about the same time."

"Olson? Isn't that the victim's name in the case you're working?"

"Good memory. Karin (with an 'i') Olson would be the younger sister of Sonja Olson, the deceased. Olson would be her maiden name. May have changed along the way."

"Do you have anything else on her?"

"No."

"That's gonna make things a bit tougher because it was so long ago. Before the age of the internet."

"I know. But finding her is absolutely vital to the case. Pull out all the stops. Use every trick and tool at your disposal."

"Why is finding her so important, Mac?"

"I'm betting she's invaluable to the wind-up of this whole thing. But finding her is only half the problem. The other half is getting her to consent to a DNA test."

"Oh, Mac, you've found something connected directly to the victim?"

"I think we have. But there's no time to waste. I need Karin Olson found, ASAP."

"No problem. I'll order takeout and work through lunch."

"Thanks, Mary."

"Is there more?"

"Is the pope Catholic?"

"Uh oh. Here it comes …"

"How would you like the day off tomorrow?"

"I'd love it. I could get in some shopping with my sister, Audrey. She's always begging me to take a day off to go shopping."

"Only if you two shop up here in Cross Point."

"They got a mall there? Sounds like an outlet kind of place."

"I need you up here, Mary. Tonight. For a special assignment."

"Tonight?"

"Yes. Close the office early and meet me at the Happy Orchard Inn at five. I'll have a room reserved for you."

"I'm staying overnight in Podunk County?"

"Best night's sleep you'll ever have. The Happy Orchard Inn guarantees it."

"Mac, we can't afford it."

"Mary, we can't afford not to. This case is too important. We're getting close."

"Now you've got me worried. What is it you want me to do?"

"No worries, Mary. I'll tell you when you get here. In the meantime, find Karin Olson. I'll see you at the Happy Orchard Inn around five."

* * * * * * * *

The pieces of a plan were beginning to coalesce. O'Malley was a wild card, but maybe he could be put to use somehow. The important thing was for him to deliver the mobile fingerprint scanner. After that, the trick would be keeping him away from Jo Hunter and the rest of the CPPD while he was in town.

The most challenging part of the plan I reserved for myself. It was also the most problematic, because ultimately it meant breaking the law in order to pursue justice for Sonja Olson and her family. I assumed trespassing was probably a minor offense in Cross Point, if I got caught, and if the college decided to press charges. But, from a law enforcement viewpoint, the ramifications of my actions while trespassing could bring severe consequences of their own.

I opened the Buckland State College brochure and spread out the campus map on my bed, rechecking the route I had chosen. Avoiding campus security was tantamount to the plan's success. Penetrating the school grounds without driving in or out would not be an issue, because BSC was essentially an open campus for pedestrians. The challenge would be avoiding the cameras and sensors in the dark.

That was the quandary I was wrestling with when Rachel telephoned me with her update.

"How did it go with your mother?"

"Seems you might be right about Shelly Hardwick. He would have been twenty-three in 1977, two years younger than brother Ryan. At the time he was a postal carrier with about five months' experience under his belt. Get this: his mail route included BSC. Mother said she would see him on campus daily, walking with his mail bag, carrying a set of faculty mailbox keys while making his deliveries."

"That's really interesting. It ties him directly to the school. Does she happen to know where he might have been on Saturday, September third?"

"No. She didn't keep track of his movements, obviously, and she had no reason to ask anyone at the time, including Ryan. But back then, mail was delivered six days a week, so there is a good chance he could have been on campus that day. Mother usually wasn't there on weekends, unless there was a special event or occasion she and father needed to attend. And classes did not officially begin that year until the following Tuesday, September sixth."

I let the information sink in a little before I spoke. "It's unlikely the Postal Service has kept weekly timesheets dating back that far, so we won't be able to place Shelly on campus during work hours in uniform on the day of the murder, unless a credible witness crawls out from under a rock after forty-four years. That ain't likely to happen and, even if it did, I don't recall seeing an exact time of death in the police report. We know Ryan Hardwick discovered the body at eleven-thirty that night, and Randall Hall was locked up around twelve-thirty earlier that day, when the last of the CPP theater troupe left. That gives us an eleven-hour window that would have partly coincided with a Saturday mail delivery."

"Was Shelly ever interviewed by police or FBI?"

"If so, it was not part of the official record I saw. Of course, we can always ask him where he was that day."

"You really think he would tell us the truth?"

"No, but it may set him off. That might be a good indicator of guilt."

"I don't want to be around him when that happens."

"You won't be. I won't let you."

"Where does that leave us? Do you still think it's necessary to keep the police out of it now that Ryan appears to be in the clear?"

"Daddy could have been mopping up after his second son instead of his first. Also, Ryan might have known or suspected his little brother was involved and looked the other way from the outset. Might account for his sudden mood swings. Did you tell Rose that we suspect Shelly?"

"No, and she didn't ask. But I'm sure she can read between the lines. Why else would we have a sudden interest in the last surviving Hardwick?"

"Here, again, it all seems to be pointing in that direction."

"So, do you still want me to have that drink with him?" I could hear the resignation in her voice. I couldn't blame her. She wanted no part in it, but she knew it was crucial to advancing the cause. I needed to push her a little, to build up her confidence.

"More than ever. One drink. Make a little pleasant conversation. You don't have to stay long or even finish your drink. It's only important that he finish his. We need the prints from his glass."

"Oh, great. How am I supposed to get them while he's sitting there?"

"You're not. Mary Porter will take care of that task. She's coming in around five this afternoon and checking in at the HOI. She'll be sitting in the bar somewhere near you by six. Her assignment is to snatch his cocktail glass once you've gone, even if she has to wait all night for the right opportunity."

"How?"

"She's smart. She'll figure it out."

"She must be quite a gal, to come all this way and risk her neck for her job."

"Neither of you will be alone. TPD is sending a detective up here to monitor the case and protect their loaned equipment. He'll be stationed in the bar, should there be any trouble."

"Has Jo Ellen been notified?"

"Not a chance."

"She may get wind of it. She has her ways, Mac."

"Not if I can help it."

"Sounds like you've thought of everything. Where are you going to be while all this is going on?"

"Collecting the necessary evidence to nail the son of a bitch!"

"You're going back to Randall Hall alone? How will get past security? Are you planning to take the piano leg with you?"

"The details are for me to work out, Rachel. The less you know about my actions tonight, the better. In legal speak, it's called plausible deniability. You can't say what you don't know."

"I don't like it."

"Neither do I, but it's the best we can do without involving the local cops. Just do your part, and don't worry about anything else. We'll all meet up afterward, say, around eleven at the Inn."

"Wish me luck."

"Don't get caught."

22

Mary arrived right at five. O'Malley trailed in ten minutes later. Neither seemed pleased despite the warm reception of gregarious innkeepers Hugh Bennett and Mark Abrams.

They were assigned Rooms 3 and 4 on the second floor, which effectively placed their sleeping quarters between Rachel's and mine. No doubt both would have appreciated the irony if they knew.

While availability at the Happy Orchard Inn was not a problem for the time being, Hugh had let Rachel know that the Presidential Suite would be needed by the weekend for a prestigious Chinese businessman and his family who were planning to tour the BSC campus. Room 7 was still closed for cleaning, but both owners were hopeful it would be ready shortly, in case Rachel's stay needed to be extended. My own stay, of course, remained on a day-to-day basis, with funds running desperately low.

After Mary and O'Malley settled in, we three met in the lobby. I briefed them on the case and then outlined the plans for the evening.

Addressing O'Malley first, I inquired, "Did you bring the mobile scanner?"

O'Malley huffed and puffed, then finally stammered, "Perkins should have his head examined but, yes, against my better judgment, I brought the scanner with me." He reached into his leather case and removed a black, triangle-shaped device about the size of a computer mouse.

"Nothing to it, Cole. Even a halfwit like you can do it."

"Your confidence in my abilities is heartwarming, O'Malley."

He gave me a disgusted look. "Now listen up. Basically, there are four buttons. Press the green 'on' button and point the 'eye' over the surface you want scanned for prints. Make sure the surface is smooth. The blue button operates the ultraviolet light. The red button turns the scanner off. When you're done scanning, the yellow button will transmit your digitized prints to the FBI's central databank. It will beep three times when the transmission is complete."

He handed me the scanner and continued.

"This device has already been encrypted with our unique registration number. Without it you'd be denied access to the FBI database. When you have a match, the identification information is sent to TPD headquarters and forwarded to my phone. That's it."

I was sufficiently impressed. "You're right. That is really simple."

"You still thinking of keeping the local force out of the loop, Cole?"

"What do you think?"

"I think it's a mistake. I'd be pissed if someone did that to us. Even with an antiquated cold case like this."

"Chief Perkins thinks differently."

"Does he? I still don't know what you have over him, Cole, but I swear one day I'm gonna find out."

"Don't trouble yourself, O'Malley. It's something you wouldn't understand. It's called trust."

"Is that a fact? Then what do you call what I'm doing here?"

"Following orders."

Mary, who had been sitting on the sofa listening to our bickering, spoke up. "Why don't you two call a truce? Your squabbling is childish. Grow up."

The force of Mary's words caught O'Malley by surprise. I could tell he wasn't used to being spoken to that way by a woman.

"Yes ma'am," he replied with a feigned salute. "How do you work with this clown?"

"Enough," I bellowed. "We've got work to do. I can put our differences aside for one night. I hope you can, too."

O'Malley made a sour face. I took that to mean he was in agreement at least temporarily. "What else do you need me to do?" he asked.

"I need you to keep an eye on Mary tonight—and another woman. This woman." I showed him a grainy headshot of Rachel, taken from one of her columns. He passed it over to Mary, who was seeing her for the first time.

"She's pretty, Mac."

"Her name is Rachel Lynwood. She will be at the bar next door, having a drink with a man named Sheldon Hardwick. One drink, that's all. When she leaves, I need you, Mary, to grab Hardwick's cocktail glass. It's his prints we're after."

"To compare with the ones you'll be lifting," O'Malley said.

"Exactly. If they match, we have our man."

"If not?" he questioned.

"We move on."

Mary looked deeply perplexed. "How do you suggest I steal this guy's glass?"

"Take it as soon as he leaves, or when he goes to the men's room. Grab it before the bartender does. Carefully. Use a tissue or a napkin, wrap it and put it in your pocketbook. Then get the hell out of there."

"What if the bartender sees?"

"Blow him a kiss and drop a twenty on the bar. That should cover it."

Mary inhaled deeply. She knew what had to be done. Done right, it could work.

"Any luck locating the sister, Karin Olson?" I asked Mary.

"I managed to find a telephone number for someone with that name, the right age, divorced, and living in Irvine, California. I'm waiting for a return call."

"Okay, great. Let's hope it's our girl."

"Where will you be while all this is happening, Mac?" asked O'Malley. I could tell it was about time for his cigarette break; his foot was tapping double time.

"On the BSC campus, surreptitiously gathering the evidence necessary to convict Hardwick of the wicked crime he committed forty-four years ago."

"I still say it's police work. Let the locals do their job, or call in the FBI," argued O'Malley.

"I agree with O'Malley," seconded Mary with a worried look.

"I can't chance it. This is a strange town. There have been rumblings about the force, innuendos that can't be ignored. Too much time has elapsed with nothing being done. Reputations are at stake. And in the final analysis, we all have to agree, 'Blood is thicker than water.'"

"When does the action begin?" asked O'Malley, leaping to his feet.

I glanced at my watch. "Now. Have your cigarette. Then treat Mary to a nice dinner at the Whistling Pines Tavern. Try the short ribs. I'll see you both back here around eleven."

* * * * * * * *

The stage was set. The plan was in motion. All that remained was my part. I flashed Rachel's alumni card and boarded the campus shuttle at six-thirty in front of the post office, taking a seat in the back of the bus. On board were two students, a boy and a girl. We picked up a third, another boy on Arbor Street, just before entering at the south gate.

I felt like a ninja, dressed head to toe in black: long-sleeve hooded sweatshirt, jeans, Converse high tops. Rachel had picked up the clothes and shoes at a nearby thrift shop. In my pockets, I carried my wallet, room key, penknife, phone, surgical gloves and a plastic sandwich bag. The fingerprint scanner was duct-taped across my stomach for safekeeping.

For show, I brought along a book—a paperback novel called *Search for the Missing Hunter* by some obscure New Jersey Pine Barrens writer. As we passed through the security checkpoint, I held the book up to my face, pretending to read. Brandon was in the guardhouse. He never gave me, or any of the other passengers, a sidelong glance.

We disembarked at the Lewis Library at ten minutes after seven. Hood up and book in hand, I bounded up the library steps, where I'd wait for the sky to grow a bit darker.

The library was open until nine. Last bus back to town was at ten. I'd be long gone before then.

I sat in the same cubicle I had during my first visit, last Thursday. Nothing had changed. The scholarly, antique smell of leather mixed with old wood still permeated the reading area. The ceiling lights were on. The interior seemed dimmer now, but comfortable. I noticed the indistinct chatter of other library visitors, then dove back into my book.

At seven-forty-five p.m., I unfolded my map and rechecked my route. The auditorium was about thirty yards away. I calculated it would take me half a minute to jog there. Less than two minutes if I walked. There was only one camera to avoid along the way, and that was right above the library front door. Giving my hood a tug, I stood and walked to the rear of Randall Hall.

◆ ❋ ❀ ❀ ❋ ◆ ◦

While I was waiting for darkness to descend, seven miles away, Rachel was waiting for her night to begin. She was anxious and wanted to get it over with.

Shelly Hardwick was late—if he was coming at all. Rachel didn't know. No one knew. She glanced up and caught her worried reflection in the mirror behind the bar. She fixed a strand of hair that had fallen out of place. Nearby sat a man and woman who had introduced themselves as the McKenzie Cole plants, sent in to assist her. Rachel had spoken to the woman, Mary Porter, over the phone. Now she gave Rachel an encouraging smile. The man in the suit, Detective Greg O'Malley, patted his gun reassuringly. She forced a small smile at both of them.

The man nodded, then turned his attention back to his appetizer.

Rachel's mind conjured all sorts of wild scenarios. She was on the verge of panic. What if Hardwick was a no-show? How long should she wait? Would she go through the exercise all over again tomorrow night, or the next?

Time slowed. Minute by minute, she nursed her Chablis, anticipating her mark's arrival. She had nearly finished her drink and contemplated ordering another when she heard a throaty male voice behind her.

"Well, whaddya know? Look who's here … again!"

Startled, Rachel looked in the mirror and saw the menacing figure of Shelly Hardwick standing behind her. O'Malley and Mary saw him, too.

He had changed from his work clothes into casual street clothes but had not taken the time to shower. He reeked. Rachel silently bestowed on him the new nickname, "Smelly" Hardwick. She felt nauseated, repulsed. But it was showtime.

She finished her wine, turned to him, and said with a half-smile, "Aren't you gonna offer to buy a girl a drink?" She moved her pocketbook from the bar stool she'd been saving for Shelly. But he didn't budge.

Rachel weighed her options.

"Okay. How about if I buy you a drink, then?" She motioned to the bartender.

"Ain't this some switcheroo," said Shelly cautiously. "Where's that guy you been leading by the nose around town?"

"He's not here, I guess. But you certainly are." She patted the seat next to her invitingly as the bartender arrived with their drinks.

"You ain't gonna run out on me again, are ya?" said Shelly, hesitantly sitting down.

Rachel didn't answer. She knew better.

He shrugged and wrapped a dirty paw around his Manhattan and said, "Bottom's up!"

◈ ❊ ◈ ◉ ◈ ❊ ◈

When I'd reached the back of Randall Hall, I took a moment to reconnoiter the area. Not a soul in sight. I approached the ladies' bathroom window and pulled open the lowest jalousie slat. Like before, the other slats fanned out. I only need one entry point, and I would take the widest possible.

The challenges were numerous. For one thing, I was not as slender as the very fit Rachel Lynwood. For another, I'd have to pull my weight up along the smooth brick wall to climb in through the window. I worried about damaging the equipment taped to my abdomen while sliding over the ledge on my belly. A younger man would not have had such issues; but a younger man was not available for the job.

So I had to think like a young man and "just do it," as they say in the Nike commercials. The trick was not to overthink it and not to stop once I got going. Gripping the ledge with both hands, I hoisted my body, my feet slipping a little as I scrambled up the brick wall. I sucked in my gut and tumbled through the opening, onto the bathroom floor.

Getting up, I checked for broken bones and damaged equipment. Aside from my scraped elbows, all seemed in order, so I made my way using my phone to light the hallway, slipping into the auditorium for the third time this week. I was beginning to feel like a cat burglar.

Up on the stage, I donned the surgical gloves Rachel had gotten for me. Bending carefully beneath the upright piano, I lifted the corner with the wobbly leg and shook it until it came loose and fell to the floor with a loud thud. Something else fell out too—crumpled paper that wedged the leg in place. It must have gotten stuck up in the shaft when Sinclair was with me.

I wasted no time getting to work. I placed my phone on top of the piano to give me some light. Next, I removed the mobile scanner from my body and switched on the green power button and blue UV button. Then, holding the leg by its tiny wheel, I slowly ran the scanner up, down, and around the leg. It looked clean to me, but I was hoping the scanner would see things I could not.

When I finished scanning for prints, I pressed the yellow button and waited for the three beeps to let me know the data was sent off to the FBI. Then I switched the unit off and re-taped it to my torso.

I removed the sandwich bag and took the penknife from my pocket, intending to scrape some of the crusted brown gunk, which I suspected was dried blood, from the bolt threads. But first I picked up the piece of paper that had been stuck to the bolt.

Carefully I unfolded it. That's when I realized I was holding no ordinary scrap but rather something unexpected and astonishing. I could tell from the printed lines, the treble clef and the music notes that it was the missing corner torn from the blood-spattered sheet music found beside the body forty-four years ago. There were more blotchy smudges of dried blood on this little piece of paper.

What a stroke of luck! Staring at it, I had a hunch this little wad was the missing link. Surely, if we could get DNA from the paper we wouldn't need the particle scrapings from the bolt. I sealed the precious piece of paper into the little plastic bag and placed it gently into my sweatshirt pouch.

I made quick work of replacing the piano leg, which, without the paper wedge was even shakier than before. I pitied the next person who sat down to play this piano!

23

Shelly put down his glass, but it surely hadn't improved his mood. "So, who is this guy? Where do you know him from?"

"I went to school with a friend of his," replied Rachel, trying to assume a casual tone.

"How does he know my brother?"

"I don't know that he does."

"I saw him at Ryan's funeral."

"What a coincidence."

"What's he doing in town?"

"Working for my mother."

"Rose? What's he doing for Rose?"

"Why don't you ask her?"

"She don't talk to me, you know that. How did you hook up with him?"

Rachel was growing weary of his questions and didn't like where they seemed to be heading. "His friend said to look me up."

"And what are *you* doing back in Cross Point?"

"Visiting my mother. What's with the fifty questions?"

"I ain't seen you around for a while."

"Well, don't get used to it. Drink up."

Rachel made her move to leave, but Shelly was quicker. He grabbed her by the arm. "Where you going? You haven't finished your drink."

"This conversation's gotten old." She tried to shake free of his grip. "Let go of me."

Shelly pulled her back more forcefully. "I ain't done talking to you."

"Well, I'm done with you."

Across the room, O'Malley was up and out of his seat. The sudden movement caught Shelly's eye, freezing him. Rachel glanced across the room, expecting to catch O'Malley's eyes. Instead, she saw Shelly's staring back at her in the mirror.

"Say, what's going on here?" barked Shelly.

O'Malley dashed around the bar in a hurry. "Let her go," he shouted, coming up behind Shelly and pinning him against the bar. Shelly released Rachel. She backed away slowly, looking across the room to see what Mary was going to do. Mary got up out of her seat, but then she suddenly stopped. A stocky policewoman stood behind Rachel, blocking her path. She drew her gun.

"Everyone stop," Chief Hunter commanded. "Stay where you are."

"Shelly was harassing me," explained Rachel. "This nice man came to my rescue."

Hunter pushed Rachel aside. "Let him go," she said to O'Malley. O'Malley didn't move. "I said to let him go," Hunter repeated. She swung O'Malley around and saw the gun in his shoulder holster. "Whoa!" She pointed her gun directly at O'Malley's face. The bar fell silent. Not a soul dared breathe. "Let him go now. I'm not gonna ask you again."

O'Malley released his hold on Shelly.

"Git," Hunter said to her uncle. "Now, Shelly!" she bellowed. He polished off his drink and bolted out the door.

Hunter reached under O'Malley's jacket and removed his gun. She stuck it in her belt.

"I'm a cop," said O'Malley, opening his jacket wider to reveal the badge on his belt. Name's O'Malley."

"So you say," said Hunter, looking at the badge. "What are you doing in my bar, in my town?"

"I can explain everything. Let's just go someplace quiet, away from these nice people. I know I can clear everything up."

"I'm sure you can, but first things first." She looked up at the bartender. He had his hands up like he was under arrest. "Ron, is my dinner ready?"

"Sure thing, Jo." He handed her a takeout bag from under the counter.

"Okay, O'Malley," she said, waving her gun at him to move. "Let's go. Outside. And be quick about it. I get ugly when my dinner gets cold."

O'Malley shot a glance back at Mary to say, "Now's your chance." But she was too late. Before Hunter and O'Malley were out the door, while all eyes were glued to the two of them, Rachel had already picked up Shelly's empty tumbler and slipped it in her pocketbook.

* * * * * * *

I stepped through the back door of Randall Hall to find them all there waiting for me: Chief Jo Ellen Hunter, Deputy Dale Matthews, Ray Chang, Brandon Leach, Detective O'Malley, Rachel, and Mary.

"Okay, Cole, let's have it," said Hunter, hands on her hips. "All of it."

I looked at Rachel but O'Malley spoke up. "They know why you're here, Cole. I had to tell them all of it."

"Matthews, search him. Then cuff him," ordered Hunter.

"What happened?" I asked, although I could have guessed.

O'Malley shrugged. "Best laid plans ..."

"That guy in the bar got rough with Rachel," volunteered Mary. "Sir Galahad here came to her rescue just as Chief Hunter walked in to pick up her takeout."

"I'm sorry," apologized Rachel as Matthews stripped me of my possessions and cuffed my hands behind my back. "It was a good plan—and almost worked."

Matthews yanked the mobile scanner off my torso and, from the feel of it, a piece of my skin with it. He handed the scanner to O'Malley.

"I sent the scans to the FBI," I said to O'Malley. "Any news?"

"Not yet," he replied.

"And there won't be," said Hunter. "Not if I have anything to do with it."

Matthews handed Chief Hunter the bag containing the scrap of sheet music.

"That's the smoking gun," I said to her. "If you're really interested in bringing justice to the Olson family, do what you want with me, but let O'Malley take that evidence back to Trenton to have the DNA analyzed."

"Not on your life, Cole. You're little game of playing Sherlock Holmes in Cross Point behind my back has just come to an end."

"My secretary can give you the number of someone who is a probable match with the victim's DNA on that piece of paper. It's a piece of the sheet music, torn in the heat of the moment to help hide the weapon used to murder Sonja Olson. That weapon has been hidden in plain sight for all these years. It's the left leg of the upright piano still standing in Randall Hall."

"Think about it, Jo Ellen," implored Rachel. "You can use modern technology to catch a criminal from forty-four years ago—someone who has gotten away with this awful crime for far too long. What are you afraid of? What are you covering up? Who are you hiding?"

"I'm the law around here, Rachel. Don't you forget that. I decide what gets investigated and what doesn't. I don't appreciate outsiders horning in on my turf."

"Is that it? Is that the whole problem?" I said. "If it is, we'll back off." I looked at O'Malley. "Both of us."

Hunter grew pensive. "I suppose you have a suspect?"

Now was the moment of truth. Should I reveal my hand or wait for the evidence to point to the obvious? Would the evidence ever be brought to light in the hands of Shelly's niece, who, although sworn to uphold the law, had not shown one iota of impartiality so far? I glanced at Mary and moved my hand to my lips, imitating taking a drink. She nodded and motioned toward Rachel. Rachel shook her head in the affirmative. They had Shelly Hardwick's prints.

"Follow the evidence, Chief Hunter. Do the right thing. Be open. Share it with the TPD. Only then will you learn the true identity of the killer, beyond a shadow of a doubt."

"I've heard enough. You can tell it to the judge. Take him away," she ordered Matthews.

24

"You have a visitor," said Dale Matthews, opening my cell door the following morning. I wondered who Mary would send to spring me. Back in Trenton, I didn't count many lawyers among my friends or work associates. So I was even more surprised when Rose Lynwood popped in behind Deputy Matthews. "You're free to go, Cole," he said, leaving the door open for us as he left.

Rose Lynwood smiled demurely, then shook her head disapprovingly. "When I hired you, Mr. Cole, I did not expect to have to bail you out of jail ... twice!"

"I thought Rachel put up the money the first time," I said, somewhat confused.

"Think again, Mr. Cole, and you can bet both will be deducted from your final fee."

"That's most considerate of you, Rose," I said facetiously. "How's Rachel holding up?"

"I can't say. I haven't been able to reach her since I spoke to her last night. She called to apprize me of your latest escapade."

She handed me my wallet and keys. "Walk with me to my car. I'll give you a ride back to the Inn."

No one stopped us as we left the station. I did not see Hunter on my way out.

"I came to tell you that I spoke to Ben Forrester, the current provost, and a few of the BSC trustees. They've agreed not to press charges against you for trespassing, provided I head up a drive to replace those obsolete bathroom windows in Randall Hall."

"That's good news!"

"Yes, but I'm afraid Jo Ellen is not as forgiving. She still intends to prosecute you for evidence tampering, which means you won't be able to leave the country for a while."

"That's good news, too," I said. "I wasn't planning on going abroad. At least she's considering what I handed over to her last night as evidence."

"What kind of evidence was it?"

"Hasn't Rachel been keeping you updated?"

"I'm paying you, Mr. Cole, not my daughter. Whatever evidence you have, I expect you to be forthcoming with me."

"As you have been with me, Rose?"

"Whatever do you mean?"

"Come on, we both know. Ryan didn't murder Sonja Olson. If you didn't know it then, you certainly must know it now."

"Speak your mind, Mr. Cole."

"You didn't hire me to find out if Ryan killed Sonja Olson; you hired me to find proof that he didn't. Why?"

"Do what you're supposed to do, Mr. Cole. Finish what you started. Find the killer."

❖ ❖ ❂ ❂ ❖ ❖

When I got back to the Inn, I found Mary waiting anxiously for me in the lobby.

"O'Malley got called back to Trenton. Maybe I should be leaving too."

"He say anything about the mobile fingerprint scan results?"

"Yes. Your prints and a guy named Johnson Sinclair came out clear as a bell. There are literally dozens of others, mostly faded, fragments and partials, unusable. Nothing concrete."

"How did you make out with the Karin Olson in Irvine?"

"She never called me back, and I don't expect she will."

"Why not?"

"Cross Point police made me turn over the info to them last night. It's in their hands now."

"And the glass with Shelly's prints?"

"Safe, I imagine. Rachel has it."

"Where is Rachel?"

"I haven't seen her. We were supposed to meet for breakfast this morning, but she never showed. I knocked on the door to her suite, but she didn't answer."

"I'm sorry I brought you all this way for nothing, Mary."

"I'm not. Your plan might have worked if that policewoman hadn't stopped in to pick up her dinner."

"We'll never know."

"O'Malley said he's going to see if Chief Perkins can rattle Hunter's cage and get some answers."

"I'm not holding out much hope for that. Hunter is a tough nut to crack, and the truth is I did go behind her back."

"Yeah, you really pissed her off."

"That seems to be something I'm good at," I said with a self-deprecating chuckle. "Pissing people off. Even Rose Lynwood is not real happy with me right now."

"If it's any consolation, Mac, I think you've won over her daughter, if that matters to you. She's a keeper."

"Yeah, but I'm not."

I gave Mary a hug for the road and a light kiss on the forehead. "Keep the home fires burning, Mary. I'll be back soon."

"Be careful, Mac."

* * * * * * *

After Mary left, I tried reaching Rachel on her cell phone. It went straight to voicemail. Next I walked over to the front desk, to inquire about her there. Mark Abrams was working behind the counter.

"Have you seen Ms. Lynwood this morning, Mark?"

"Can't say that I have. It does seem a bit odd. She's been an early riser during her stay."

"Yes, I agree. Any messages for me?"

He looked around and under the counter. Then he checked my cubbyhole and hers. "Doesn't appear to be any."

That left me only one other option. "Say, Mark, I wonder if I can ask you a favor?"

"Shoot."

"Would you mind coming with me and opening her room? Maybe she's left a note for me there."

Together we scoured the room but came up empty—almost. I did happen to notice that, wherever Rachel went, she left in a hurry, without taking the time to fold and put away her pajamas or make her bed. From what I knew about Rachel Lynwood and her structured upbringing, she was much neater than that.

I left Mark and went around back to check the parking lot. Rachel's cream VW was still sitting where she had parked it the day before. Something was definitely amiss. I was beginning to worry. After last night had dissolved into total chaos, and after spending the balance of the night in the Cross Point jail, I would have expected Rachel to come see me first thing. I felt we had grown that close in our relationship. The fact that no one had seen her, including Rose, Mary, and Mark, troubled me deeply.

On a whim, I marched across the street to the post office, intending to have my showdown with Sheldon Hardwick. It had been a long time coming, and if he had "roughed up" Rachel in the bar last night, as I'd been told, he had better be ready for a face full of McKenzie Cole rage. I may have been handcuffed on the case, quite literally, but I was not through with Shelly Hardwick.

The surprises kept coming. Shelly was not at work. I learned from a coworker that he had called out sick—a rarity, she commented. Concern gripped me. The hairs on the back of my neck stood up. My instincts told me something terrible was on the wind.

My very next thought was to rush over to Shelly Hardwick's house and break down the door. The coworker grudgingly gave me the address, but before I could get to my car, my cell phone rang.

"Cole, it's Hunter."

"What did I do this time?"

"I owe you an apology."

"For what?"

"Your police work. It seems, despite my misgivings, you are fairly intuitive."

"Go on."

"I had the DNA on that scrap of sheet music analyzed. Seems you were right. It's Sonja Olson's."

"Are you sure?"

Dave Hart

"The woman in Irvine that your secretary found. She's the sister. We got a positive match."

I couldn't contain my excitement. "I knew it!"

"Wait. There's more. Those dark smudges were her blood too, lots of it, with fingerprints belonging to the one who balled up the paper and stuck it up under the piano leg. The killer. We know who it is."

"I'm listening."

"We got a match on the prints from his house. I just left there. Same as the prints on the glass Rachel took from the bar. She gave it to me voluntarily last night, in an effort to bargain for your release."

"Did you arrest him?"

"No. I didn't get the results until this morning. He was already gone. But you might know where he went. Cole, I fear Rachel may be in danger. We found her laptop and iPad at the house. He may be planning to eliminate all the loose ends that have come unraveled. That might have included you, if I hadn't kept you in the Cross Point pokey overnight."

"Gee, thanks.

"Cole, can you think of anyone else who knows what you know, besides Rachel, now that you've resurrected the case? Does Rose know?"

"No."

"You sure?"

"Yes."

"Anyone else, a name he might be able to beat out of her?"

I was about to answer no, but then one person who had been most reluctant but also most helpful popped into my head.

"Yes, but you're gonna need me to show you the way. His property is not easy to find."

25

I tried phoning Johnson Sinclair to warn him, but he didn't answer. If he truly had ESP, I sure as hell hoped it was working for him now.

Hunter picked me up in her patrol car. I sat in the back while Matthews drove, and Hunter relayed my directions from the shotgun seat.

"I had a nice Zoom chat with your Chief Perkins earlier this morning," she said by way of small talk. I had already noticed a change in her demeanor toward me on our earlier call. "I told him I didn't appreciate his department helping you do an end run around my exposed flank. I thought the two of you were trying to grab some headlines at my expense."

"I'm glad he clarified everything for you."

"Oh, he did. Only, I'm not sure which is more painful: TDP's shot at the glory in solving the cold case, or your mistrust of my guys and me. In Italy it's a crime to insult the police."

"Just ask Amanda Knox," Matthews added with a snicker.

"You have to admit." I said, "nepotism runs deep within the CPPD through the Hardwick line, and this thing has been kept under wraps for an awful long time, if not without help from anyone."

"I admit it has in the past, but that's ended with me. Leastways Uncle Sheldon was never part of the 'brothers in blue' in-crowd. He was always the black sheep—in more ways than one."

"Do you think your grandfather or your Uncle Ryan had an inkling he might be involved in the Olson murder?"

"I can't say for certain whether they suspected Shelly or not. I can only say that, somewhere along the way, Uncle Ryan crossed a line and did something that didn't sit well with Pop-Pop Lionel."

"That's why Ryan got passed over for the promotion?"

"Evidently."

"And your mother never said anything to you?"

"She never thought much of either of her two brothers. Ryan, in particular, had a reputation around women, most of whom were my mother's friends."

"Including Rose Lynwood?"

"Rose was the love of his life. My mother said he never got over her dumping him for stuffy old Carter Lynwood. There were rumors they carried on after she remarried. But it could have been wishful thinking, or him just talking. All that was before my time."

"Just like the Olson case. So why have you kept the clamp down on the records after all this time?"

"Old wounds smell rotten, especially left to fester."

"The military has taught you well."

"It's called self-preservation, Cole. You learn to look out for yourself. Kill your own skunks."

"It must be even harder for a woman."

"If that's all a man sees, yes."

"So, what kind of agreement did you and Chief Perkins come to regarding the Olson case?"

"I consented to his department's shadow oversight of our investigation as long as we got full credit for the collar. And of course, your name never gets mentioned."

"Of course. TPD has always treated me like I don't exist anyway."

We reached the end of our long overdue conversation at about the same time the squad car reached the end of the long mountainside road to Johnson Sinclair's Shangri-La.

"That's his place, straight ahead," I said, pointing through the windshield.

"And that's Uncle Sheldon's F-150 parked in the driveway," Hunter added ominously. "Whatever you do, Cole, stay behind us. Don't try to be a hero."

She didn't need to tell me twice. I wasn't the hero type, especially when guns were involved. Puppy dogs caught in bear traps, maybe. That was the extent of my heroism.

We parked on a curve about fifty yards from the front porch, hoping we had not been spotted. We spread out and crept slowly toward the door with Hunter in the lead. Both Hunter and Matthews had their guns drawn. I had only my wits, but I figured it was a fair fight—as long as the other two went first.

We got to the porch and nothing stirred. Hunter motioned to Matthews to try the door. It opened easily with a dull, creaking moan. He stepped back and waited.

"Johnson Sinclair," Hunter called. "You in there? This is the police."

We waited several seconds for a response and got none. Hunter motioned for us to stay behind her as we three stealthily slipped inside the doorway.

It was dark like I remembered. The smell of jasmine incense and extinguished candles permeated the house. Several windows were open, and a steady mountain breeze blew through the séance room where I had first encountered Sinclair. His fortune telling table with its large luminous crystal ball sat in the center of the room, untouched.

Hunter motioned for me to stay put. She directed Matthews to check the upstairs rooms while she searched the first floor. After several minutes everyone reunited in the foyer.

"There's no one here," Matthews said.

"Well, they've got to be somewhere," countered Hunter. She turned to me. "What's out back?"

"Nothing, as far as I know. I never got that far."

We pushed out through the back door together and looked around. "There," I said, pointing to the path leading away from the house and up into the hills. "That's Sinclair's blue beret. He's never without it."

"Let's see where it leads," said Hunter.

"I know where it goes," replied Matthews. "It leads to Ribbontop Ridge, a cliff that overlooks a sheer forty-foot drop down into the Great Gorge. I used to fish and hunt near there when I was a kid."

"That's got to be their destination," I concurred. "If Shelly aims to rid himself of the reminders of his murderous past, that seems like the most logical place. One push and he's free of Rachel and Sinclair forever."

"We better hurry," agreed Hunter.

We followed the narrow, rocky path for about two hundred yards. It led straight to Ribbontop Ridge. Sheldon Hardwick stood on the precipice with his two hostages, bound and gagged, their backs to the deep chasm. He was wielding a large muleskinner's knife, poking and taunting them with it.

"Leave them be, Shelly" Hunter barked, raising her gun. "Put the knife down and back away, nice and easy. No one needs to get hurt."

"Haven't you done enough damage for one lifetime?" I asked contemptuously.

"Zip it, Cole," Hunter said to me in a stage whisper. "Don't give him a reason to go off." I took her to mean it literally, that he might take his hostages with him.

Rachel's eyes were as large as gumdrops. She was scared, and who could blame her? Sinclair, on the other hand, seemed eerily calm and relaxed. Had he seen this encounter coming? Did he have something up his sleeve?

"Think about it, Shelly," Hunter continued patiently. "There's nowhere to run, no place to hide. This all comes to an end now."

"You won't use that gun on me, Jo. I'm family."

"I'm also the law."

"Because you're a Hardwick. You'd be nothing if not for your bloodline."

"Right now, I'm dealing with some bad blood that's not feeling much like family. Come in quietly, and maybe we can talk things through."

"Too late for that, Jo." He pointed the knife at Rachel and Sinclair. "These people know something bad I done." He pointed the knife my way. "Him too, the nosy bastard. Couldn't leave well enough alone, could you?"

"Don't make it worse for yourself, Shel," said Hunter, undeterred. "I know what they know, what you've kept secret for all these years. What you've kept from the family. Time to pay the piper."

"Never! You don't know what it was like back then. You weren't around. It was awful being me."

"Don't make it worse than it already is. We ... *I* can fix this. But only if you drop the knife and come with me now."

"What's done is done. You can't change the past. You can't make it go away. She was beautiful and talented. I wanted her so badly. But she resisted. She rejected me like all the rest."

Hunter must have realized trying to reason with her uncle was getting her nowhere. She needed a secondary strategy. She motioned with her head for Matthews to fan out. He began circling wide from the left. She glanced my way. I acknowledged by circling slowly to the right, making like a claw, closing in on Shelly from three sides. I was unarmed and would have to improvise if he came at me.

It was obvious Hunter didn't want to shoot her uncle unless he left her no other choice. But where was that tipping point? I wondered. Because, to me, as long as Shelly held the knife and kept his hostages on the edge of the cliff, Rachel and Sinclair were in imminent danger of being forced over the side. If they made a run for it, one of them might escape. Ah, but which one? That same thought probably kept each frozen in place while they waited for Hunter to come up with a better plan.

But Shelly was not a complete fool. He recognized his niece's gambit. Ignoring Sinclair, he grabbed Rachel by the hair, pulled her head back, and raised the knife to her throat. Matthews and I stopped dead in our tracks. Sinclair inched off to one side, apparently no longer a concern to Shelly.

"Stop!" Shelly shouted.

Everyone halted. Guns were inoperable now. A shot might accidentally hit Rachel. The force might send both Rachel and Shelly backward over the cliff. Rachel was petrified. I felt totally useless. I sensed we all did.

Except for Sinclair. No longer commanding Shelly's attention, he stopped inching away. Suddenly, he changed course and ran directly at Shelly's blind side, knocking him sideways. The knife fell, Shelly and Rachel tumbled to the ground, and Rachel rolled out of harm's way.

Hands tied and mouth gagged, Sinclair climbed on top of Shelly, but Shelly bucked him off. Sinclair rolled toward the edge of the cliff. With a kick, Shelly drove Sinclair's lower half over the edge. In a gesture of desperation, Sinclair reached up and hooked his bound arms around Shelly's foot, hoping to gain purchase. Instead, he took Shelly with him. The two men slid over the edge, into the abyss.

26

Rachel buried her head in my chest, muffling her soft sobs. I put an arm around her and held her as close as propriety would permit in the back of a squad car. Chief Hunter was on the radio with the Allegheny authorities, informing them of two bodies at the bottom of Great Gorge. "Murder-suicide. The killer is one of the victims. He's also the primary suspect in a Cross Point cold case. A full report will follow."

"Poor guy," said Hunter, wistfully referring to Sinclair. "I thought you would be the one to try and play hero today, Cole."

"Not me, Chief. I know better. I get a touch of vertigo just from standing at the top of a staircase."

Rachel lifted her head, tears flooding her pretty emerald eyes. "Sinclair saved my life, Mac. He sacrificed his life for mine. Why would he do that?"

"I'm no expert in human behavior, but if I were to venture a guess, I'd say we just witnessed the demise of two tormented souls: one by what he did a long time ago, the other by what he saw in his visions that no one else saw. Neither would have been happy until their demons were laid to rest. That's what happened today.

"Sinclair lived alone with his gift in a kind of surreal silence. That's the hand he was dealt. The 'curse,' he called it. Today he took matters into his own hands, no doubt knowing how it would end up."

"Are you saying you think he saw himself going over that cliff?"

"How could he not? He could read the future, every minute of every day of his life."

"What do you think, Jo Ellen?" asked Rachel. "How would the police academy categorize the psychological profile of Uncle Shelly?"

"There isn't a simple label, as far as I know. He was never a particularly pleasant person to deal with, it's true, but that doesn't necessarily make him a bad person."

"Nor does it excuse the awful crime he committed forty-four years ago," Rachel argued.

"Agreed. That was one hell of a screw-up. Nasty and totally unforgivable. He should have been locked up—and would have been, if he'd gotten caught. That doesn't seem to matter much anymore."

"It does to me," said Rachel.

"Me too," Matthews chimed in.

"It matters to the Olson family," I added, "wherever they are. And it matters to the people of Cross Point, to the students, faculty and administrators of BSC."

Hunter sighed. "I don't disagree with any of you. All I'm saying is the case can now be closed. But was justice served?"

"Another life was lost!" Matthews pointed out.

"Exactly. And for what? What if you had let sleeping dogs lie, Cole? Johnson Sinclair would still be alive."

"I couldn't do that. Besides, it wasn't up to me. I was hired to do a job. Unlike Sinclair, or maybe even you, Jo, I never know how a case is going to end."

"I'll bet it's not usually good."

"That's always going to be true for someone," I countered. "Being right doesn't always help the person who was wronged."

Hunter grew pensive. "Still, for the life of me, I can't think of another time Shelly had a run-in with the law."

I couldn't help but challenge her. "And that bothers you? After what we saw him do today?"

"Yes, I know it shouldn't, but if he'd broken the law doing something else, we would have got right on it and maybe nabbed him long before now."

"I doubt it," I said.

"I don't." She seemed adamant. "We're not the same department we were forty years ago."

"You mean you don't have your heads in the sand?"

"You could have said up our ass."

"Same difference. How do you know Pop-Pop Lionel didn't sweep something under the rug before you joined the force?"

"He was too busy mopping up after Ryan."

"For what?"

"Women came out of the woodwork with all sorts of accusations against him. None of them were ever prosecuted, that I know of. Never enough proof. Most of the women backed down when the hard questions were asked."

"That's incredible. You consider that a Hardwick victory?"

"I don't know what the truth is, Cole. I never bothered to ask. I was away in the service for some of it. It stopped by the time I made the squad."

I looked over at Rachel. "Did you ever hear anything about Ryan's activities from Rose or your father?"

"Father forbade us from speaking his name in the house. I guess that's because he never really liked being Mother's second choice. That was my impression, anyway."

"Enough of this Ryan nonsense. Let me ask you something, Cole. Are you satisfied with the job you did?"

"Don't you mean, will my client be satisfied? We'll see. That depends on what she was really looking for."

"What are you going to tell her?" Hunter wanted to know.

"The truth. That her first husband Ryan Hardwick did not murder Sonja Olson forty-four years ago. His brother Shelly Hardwick did. And if Ryan knew or Lionel knew, they took it to their graves. Now Shelly is in one, too, but the truth is known."

Hunter scrutinized my response, studying me in the rearview mirror. "You still seem troubled. What bothers you about the case?"

"We have the murder weapon. We know who the killer was. But what was Shelly's motive?"

"We may never know the real reason," offered Matthews as he turned onto Main Street. We passed a sign that read "Welcome To Cross Point: Population 46,163."

"Forty-six thousand, one hundred sixty-*two*," he said under his breath.

"It was a crime of passion involving a deranged man, pure and simple," offered Rachel, unsolicited. She had regained her vitality and feistiness during the long ride back.

"Is that the kind of person Sheldon Hardwick was?" I asked Hunter directly.

She answered the question based, I assumed, on what she knew or perhaps from what she'd been told by her mother or others growing up.

"He was a boy who was abandoned by his long-suffering mother, who died before he reached his potential. He was a man who could never measure up to his father's expectations. A man who never married, for one reason or another. And a man who lived, green with envy, in the shadow of his older brother's camaraderie with men and prowess with women."

"That's one damaged dude," Rachel said, "and then he became a postal worker, to boot."

Hunter nodded. "That was Sheldon Hardwick."

27

I turned into the drive at Seventeen Sycamore, careful to avoid the shedding sycamores, around four in the afternoon, nearly a full week after my first visit to the stately Lynwood home. My Jaguar was packed, the Happy Orchard Inn was paid in full, and I was ready to return to Trenton for some much-needed R&R. All that remained was to settle up with the "little old lady" who had hired me over the phone and convinced me to attend the funeral of a total stranger in pursuit of gainful employment. In the end, I had to admit, the case did not disappoint.

Rachel had wanted desperately to come along, but I convinced her that, since her mother alone had hired me, it was my responsibility to give my final accounting to her alone, in person. Besides, Chief Hunter needed Rachel to go down to the station to claim the personal property that was stolen from her room at HOI and recovered in Sheldon Hardwick's home.

I was relieved on many levels when she finally let me go without her. Nevertheless, I invited her to come to Trenton anytime for a night out at Jake's Joint, where she could reunite with Nick Falcone while the two of us regaled him with tales of our recent exploits—sans a few intimate details.

It was another glowing, warm afternoon in tree-filled Cross Point, Pennsylvania— the kind that made this Jersey boy appreciate the good things in a life that we sometimes take for granted. Lovely Rose Lynwood, gracious as ever, was waiting for me as she was the first time on her porch, with an ice-cold pitcher of homemade mint tea at the ready.

She greeted me with a coquettish smirk. "I do declare, I'm going to hate to see you leave, Mr. Cole."

I accepted the glass of tea she offered with a heartfelt smile.

"Oh, why's that, Rose?"

"Because of the entertainment value, of course. I don't believe I have ever seen my daughter so happy. You've certainly made good use of her time while you've been here."

"The feeling's definitely mutual. She was a big help and a jolly companion. Without her I never would have been able to find out what you asked me to find out."

I handed her the expense account Mary had prepared at the office and faxed to me at the Inn.

"Hmm," she said, mulling over the two-page report. She took out her checkbook and wrote me a check for the amount specified. "Everything seems to be in order," she said, handing me the check.

I was flabbergasted. I expected an argument for some of the entries, like the dinner and breakfasts for two. At the very least, I expected her to deduct the bail bond and parking fine she'd paid for me. In total, she waived close to two thousand dollars.

"So, what exactly did you find out for me, Mr. Cole?"

"The Olson cold case has been solved and put to rest. In the next few weeks, the Cross Point prosecutor's office will confirm the physical evidence collected on this case is sufficient to convict Sheldon Hardwick, deceased, for the 1977 murder of a twenty-five-year-old music major at BSC named Sonja Olson.

I read to her the following excerpt from a draft of Chief Hunter's police report:

"On September 3, 1977, between the hours of two and five p.m., 'Shelly,' as he was known, used his job as a letter carrier for the United States Postal Service to gain access to the grounds of Buckland State College, where he came upon Ms. Sonja Olson, alone, living surreptitiously in Randall Hall.

"He found her playing the piano naked, performing music from the then-popular Broadway musical 'Hair' in the cast's nude style. When she repeatedly rebuffed his inappropriate advances, he bound and gagged her, then proceeded to beat her upon the face and head mercilessly until she was dead, using the loose wooden piano leg he had removed from the upright piano. Later, using a torn section of the sheet music, he would clean and restore the leg to the upright piano, where it remained hidden in plain sight for all these many years, the case unresolved.

"In June of this year, working in collaboration with the Trenton Police Department, Cross Point Police under the leadership of Chief Jo Ellen Hunter responded to a tip regarding the condition of the aging piano and, using current analysis technology, determined unequivocally that fingerprints and DNA samples taken from the piano leg and dating back forty-four years to the criminal homicide did indeed belong to the killer Sheldon Hardwick and his victim, Sonja Olson. Recently, while attempting to evade

capture and stand trial for his crime, Sheldon Hardwick plunged to his death from Ribbontop Ridge in Allegheny, Pennsylvania, taking another innocent victim, property owner Johnson Sinclair, with him."

Rose listened carefully to the report, rocking in her wicker rocking chair to the cadence of my reading voice. When I had finished, she sat back in her chair and stared directly at me.

"Is this what I paid you for, Mr. Cole? To catch the killer?"

"I go where the trail leads."

"But there is no mention of either you or my daughter in this account."

"It's what we agreed to with the CPPD. Hopefully, Rachel will be more forthcoming about our involvement in her book and include the insightful assistance of Johnson Sinclair."

"But surely that will be considered a work of fiction. The CPPD has the goods in place. Their account will be on file as 'official.'"

"No doubt that will be the case, Rose."

"Well, for what it's worth, I am thankful for the crack police work, whoever did the job. I'm sure the Olson family will be grateful to have closure after all this time. I sure hope there is someone yet alive among them who can appreciate it."

"The victim has a sister. I've been informed she's alive and well, living in California."

Rose continued without further acknowledgment of the living Olson.

"And, of course, the college will be plenty solicitous to finally put this awful tragedy to bed and shut down the venomous internet prattle. All that remains is for the school to acknowledge it occurred. Now that it's resolved and established that the deed was done by someone outside the school community, maybe the powers that be at the college will deign to put up a plaque in memory of this poor unfortunate girl. May she rest in peace."

"That would be nice," I said, and I meant it.

"Where does that leave us, exactly, Mr. Cole? You and me and the bill I just paid for your detective work?"

"I believe you already know the answer to that, Rose. You hired me to prove Ryan Hardwick murdered Sonja Olson. Or did you? That's what you said in our original meeting. But I didn't do that. In actuality, I think what you really meant was for me to prove beyond a doubt that he *didn't* kill Sonja Olson. You didn't want to believe it, and you had to know for sure before you left this world."

"Go on."

"Went I first came onboard, you pushed hard that he was guilty. Maybe too hard, I thought at the time. All I had to do was find the proof. But you hoped all along that he was innocent, and that was the proof you were really looking for. That was the proof you wanted me to find, since the police couldn't find it, and you were fearful they never would. When I realized this, I asked myself, *Why? Why is she so eager to get Ryan off the hook?*"

"And, Mr. Cole?" prompted Rose, baiting me to reveal what I knew. Waiting patiently to hear the words she had longed to hear for the last forty-four years. "What conclusion have you come to?"

"That you loved him, Rose. Still do. And he loved you. The murder of the co-ed scared you. It frightened you because you suspected Ryan might actually have done it. Surely, the opportunity was there for him. You were aware of his fondness for women and them for him. But you thought he gave them up for you. And I believe he did. But he got kinky in his exclusivity, and that scared you too. So, you bolted. You divorced him and ran to a man you thought could give you the stability you desired most in life."

Rose began rocking again slowly, her eyes fixed on me.

"Except Carter Lynwood couldn't give you *everything*, could he, Rose? There was something missing. And as time went on, it became more and more apparent that maybe you had made a mistake.

"During that time, Ryan must have sworn to you on a stack of bibles that he was innocent. He must have said over and over again that he still loved you. His family knew it. Jo Ellen Hunter told that me today. You were the love of his life. He was devastated when you left him for Carter. Crushed.

"So he went back to his old ways, his wild ways, hoping to purge you from his mind. But it was too late. He realized he couldn't have you, and you couldn't have him, not as husband and wife, never again, not in this tiny Peyton Place. But perhaps there was something you could do for each other that would forever seal your love."

Rose Lynwood leaned forward in her chair. She closed her eyes and clasped her hands to her face, sobbing softly. I stood and, like a compassionate priest hearing confession from a penitent sinner, I rested a hand gently on her bowed head and said, "Now that you know her real father isn't a killer, all that remains is for you to tell Rachel the truth."

The End

Printed in the United States
by Baker & Taylor Publisher Services